THE CREATIC

BOOKS BY ADAM PFEFFER

Published by iUniverse:

KOLAK OF THE WEREBEASTS
TWILIGHT OF THE GODS
THE MISSING LINK
TO CHANGE THE WORLD
AND OTHER STORIES
THE DAY THE DREAM CAME TRUE
AND OTHER POEMS
THE VISITORS
THE CREATION OF GOD

THE CREATION OF GOD

ADAM PFEFFER

iUniverse, Inc.
New York   Bloomington

The Creation of God

This is a work of fiction. All of the characters, names, incidents,
organizations, and dialogue in this novel are either the products
of the author's imagination or are used fictitiously.

iUniverse books may be ordered through booksellers or by contacting:

iUniverse
1663 Liberty Drive
Bloomington, IN 47403
www.iuniverse.com
1-800-Authors (1-800-288-4677)

ISBN: 978-1-4502-1255-7 (sc)
ISBN: 978-1-4502-1256-4 (ebook)

Printed in the United States of America

iUniverse rev. date: 03/10/2010

An honest God is the noblest work of man.

R.G. INGERSOLL, 1876

∴

What is it: is man only a blunder of God, or God only a blunder of man?

F.W. NIETZSCHE, 1889

Part One

1

THE MIRROR FELL to the floor with a resounding crash.

"*Ei-yeow!*"

Harry stared at the gleaming shards of glass, and groaned. "Dear God, what have I done?" he screamed, his hands grabbing at his throat.

He reached down into one of his pockets, removed a pinch of salt, and threw it over his shoulder. He quickly turned around, and looked behind him. "At least, the Devil's gone," he said with a sigh. "Must have gotten him right in the eyes."

He moved his fingers to the necklace hanging around his neck, and touched one of the beads. Most of the beads were amber, but the bead Harry touched was blue.

"Touch blue, and your wish will come true," he mumbled.

He then looked down again at the broken pieces of glass scattered over the bathroom floor. He bent down, and began picking them up one by one. One of the pieces cut his right index finger, drawing blood. "It's starting already," he moaned. "I couldn't take seven years of it."

Placing the pieces on a sheet of paper, he walked over to the sink and washed his finger. He wrapped a bandage around it, and sighed. "Might not be as bad as I thought," he said to himself, tapping his left pocket. "Good thing I found that acorn."

He walked back to the pieces of glass, and carefully picking up the sheet of paper and an old silver spoon, shuffled to the back door. He was soon walking across the yard towards a patch of dirt glistening in the moonlight. He knelt down and began digging a hole with the spoon. When he was done, he placed the pieces of glass at the bottom and covered them with dirt.

"Only way to avoid seven years of bad luck," he smiled to himself.

He was stepping back inside his house when he heard someone knocking at the door.

"Must be Donovan," he said, hurrying through the hallway.

When he opened the door, a tall man with dark hair stood there for a moment, and then stepped inside.

"What the hell have you been doing, Stanfield?" he asked, looking down at Harry's shirt. There were small dirt stains zigzagging down the front.

Harry instinctively ran his hands across the material. "Just trying to avoid some bad luck," he finally said. "You see—"

Donovan began to laugh. "You must be the most superstitious person I've ever met," he said. "It's really hard to believe that you're a man of learning. Then again, I guess we're all somewhat superstitious in our own way. I guess this whole project has something to do with our basically superstitious nature. Why, it seems to me God is probably just an old superstition."

"What about the project?" Harry anxiously asked.

"Coming along rather nicely," Donovan replied with a smile. "We're just about ready to unveil the world's fastest supercomputer to handle the project."

"Then you think we'll actually be able to do it?"

"I assure you, Harry, it'll be better than any God we've ever prayed to in the history of the human race. Why, think of it, we'll be able to create a God based on all our previous beliefs. When we get through with Him, He'll be equal to any Being that has existed for six thousand years."

Harry smiled. "Yes, yes, based on everything we hoped and dreamed about Him," he said. "I am so looking forward to help program Him."

"Should be very soon, Harry," Donovan said. "He'll be the very Being we always thought was out there. He'll be just, yet firm, and listen to everything we want to tell Him. Yes, just as we had imagined."

"The fastest supercomputer ever, right, Donovan?"

"You got it, Harry, 360 gigaflops. That's equal to 360 trillion calculations per second."

"Should be good enough to fill our needs," Harry said, smiling. "And it will contain all the Bibles of the world, and all our accepted beliefs of what constitutes the Lord."

✦
✦ ✦

"That's right, Harry. Better than the real thing ever could have been."

"When do we open the website?"

"Sooner than you think. All we have to do is make sure the computer's ready to answer any theological question someone might have. We've got to be sure it will be as authentic as possible."

"I'll get my coat, and we can get going," Harry said, walking to the closet. He pulled out a large green overcoat, and hurriedly put it on.

Donovan noticed Harry's hand slide down into one of the pockets.

"Don't tell me you have a rabbit's foot in there," he said.

"Something better," Harry replied with a grin. "Four-leaf clover. Somebody sent it to me all the way from Ireland."

"No doubt," mumbled Donovan. "Anyway, with you on the team, Harry, I have nothing but confidence that this project will be an enormous success."

Harry smiled, and with the fingers of his right hand gently rubbing the four-leaf clover, headed for the door.

✦
✦ ✦

Harry sat down at the computer terminal, and began typing at the keyboard.

"God, why is there so much misery in the world?"

He waited for a moment, and a reply soon flashed on the screen.

"Humans have so willed it. Was not Adam and Eve given the chance to live in the Garden of Eden? And did they not eat from the tree of knowledge?

✦
✦ ✦

And so, I said to Adam, 'Because thou hast harkened unto the voice of thy wife, and hast eaten of the tree, of which I commanded thee, saying, Thou shalt not eat of it: cursed is the ground for thy sake; in sorrow that shalt thou eat of it all the days of thy life.' But sin is not forever. I have given humans the free will to decide for themselves their own fate. Still, humans seem to prefer to partake of the forbidden fruit. Is that not the nature of the human being? It is only logical that misery will result."

Harry sat back and smiled. After a moment, he began typing once again.

"I am an eight-year-old boy, and I wanted to know why my sister died. She was only six. Why God?"

He hit the enter key, and waited anxiously for the reply. A few moments later, the words flashed on the screen.

"Death is just another part of life. One of the reasons I created it was to make sure I had enough angels to help me with my work. Your sister's death, while tragic to the living of the mortal world, is a blessing to those who reign in Heaven. Every death has a reason, a purpose, and your sister's death is no exception. She will be of help to me, and will do far greater things in Heaven than she ever could have done on earth. Be happy that her work in Heaven will help others down on earth. And, some day, you will see her again. She will be here in Heaven to greet you when it is your time to come. And then, you too, shall help me with my work. Until that time, have faith that everything that happens has a reason. Though you might not understand it right now, you will come to realize it in time. Just have faith in my judgment, for ye are all important to me, both small and great."

A smile inched its way across Harry's face. It was definitely almost ready. No doubt about it. A living God who would be able to answer any theological or philosophical question one might have. The only thing it couldn't do was actually create life.

Harry thought for a moment, and then began typing another question. This one, he decided, would be one that would require diplomacy. It would favor one religion's concept of God against all the other religions. He wanted to see how Project God would handle it.

"Was Jesus Christ your son?"

There was a pause, and Harry anxiously waited for the answer. After a few moments, words finally appeared on the screen.

"Jesus was my son, and yet, not my only son. You are all my children. The children of God. And while Jesus helped to spread my Word on earth, he was surely not the only one. I have sent many representatives. There were Moses, Mohammed, Buddha, Shiva, Vishnu, Confucius, Lao Tzu, and many others. All have helped to reveal my Word, and have allowed my children to become witnesses to my Work. All that matters is that you keep my Laws here on earth. It is then I will reveal the true Wisdom of the Universe, and you will all experience enlightenment, no matter which of my representatives you care to follow."

Harry nodded his head. Yes, yes, Project God was almost ready. There was only one test left. The computer had to face a few religious leaders before they could begin. If they gave it their approval, everything would work out just fine. If they decided to disapprove of the project, they would have to decide what to do next. As far as Harry was concerned, their approval didn't matter any longer. He was satisfied the computer was as real a God as they would ever get. But it was the investors he was worried about. Without religious approval, they may decide to back out of the project leading to its inevitable demise. The thought caused Harry to begin rubbing his four-leaf clover hidden away in one of his pockets. He wanted this project to succeed more than anything in the world.

"So what do you think, Harry?" asked Donovan, suddenly appearing from behind.

The suddenness of the question almost made Harry pluck out one of the clover leaves. Pulling his hand out of his pocket, Harry turned around, trying to forget his concern.

"If you ask me, Donovan, this project is as ready as it'll ever be. It's just a shame that it could be killed by a few sanctimonious windbags."

Donovan smiled. "You just let me worry about the windbags,

Harry," he said. "As long as we're all satisfied, this project's not going to die so easily. These sanctimonious windbags have only so much power. You let me worry about them."

Harry nodded his head, hoping Donovan would be true to his words. "Thanks, Donovan," he said.

✦
✦ ✦

"A most blasphemous project," Reverend Carey was saying as he looked around the Project God computer room. "You're telling me you're going to pass this piece of machinery off as the Lord?"

"At least, humans will have some contact with God," said a voice from behind. "The real God doesn't seem to want to have anything to do with people."

Reverend Carey quickly turned to see who was speaking. Harry Stanfield looked at him, and smiled.

"For your information, the Lord has many personal relationships with those who truly believe," said the Reverend. "Now I see what kind of people are working on this scandalous project."

"But you must admit—"

"That'll be all, Harry," Donovan said, cutting him off. "This is my project, and I'll handle it my own way."

Harry could see the Reverend frowning, and wished that he could tell him how he really felt about organized religion. Instead, he watched as Donovan began whispering to him as they walked away. Maybe Donovan could keep himself under control. As far as Harry was concerned, the reverend had no right to criticize the project. Why, their little project could do more to help people than hundreds of sanctimonious windbags. They not only could provide faith, they could put people in direct contact with a Lord of some kind. That was something all those windbags combined couldn't do.

He watched as another one of them was ushered through the door. A rabbi this time, wearing a yarmulke and a long, gray beard. He began to wonder what his objection would be to the project.

"This is your God?" the rabbi asked after a few minutes. "I hope you don't intend to use the real Lord's name in vain."

"No, no, rabbi," Donovan replied. "This God will be here just to answer any questions anyone might have."

"But will he give the right answers?" the rabbi said.

"That will be for you to decide. You see, we've programmed him with all the various religions, and are confident he will respond appropriately no matter who will be asking the question."

"That I would like to see," the rabbi said with a laugh.

"You're not the only one," Reverend Carey added. "I would like to know how one computer will be able to satisfy so many people of different faiths."

"That's why you're here, reverend," Donovan replied. "So you can sit down there at one of the terminals, and find out for yourself if this project has any merit."

The reverend nodded, and then Donovan led him to one of the many terminals situated on black desks throughout the room. He sat down, and then after a few moments of thought, began typing a question.

"How is one forgiven for sins committed here on earth?" the reverend typed with a smile.

There was an immediate gurgling, and then a moment later, words began appearing on the screen.

"There are many ways one may atone for one's sins," it read. "Through faith, whichever faith one chooses, one may put his or her trust in the wisdom of the Lord. Through prayer and thought, the Lord will eventually determine the motive behind one's sins, and therefore, determine whether absolution is possible. Another way to be forgiven is by undertaking works or labors that may benefit the planet in general, or one's fellow beings. The works or labors are determined by the individual, intended to contribute to the glory of the Lord, and to be undertaken at great sacrifice to the individual's material concerns. These are two of the ways to be forgiven for one's sins. It is through compassion that the Lord understands, and the individual seeks salvation."

The reverend read the words with great interest, and then somewhat surprised, began typing once again.

"Is not salvation gained by the acceptance of Jesus Christ as your Son and Savior of the world?"

There was another gurgling, and a moment later, another answer appeared.

"Jesus is but one of the many names given to my children. He is important to me, and yet, so are the many others who have spread my Word, and have succeeded in bringing about spiritual progress. I do not favor one over the other, but embrace all of them as representatives and prophets who furthered awareness and compassion."

The reverend stared at the words, gritted his teeth, and then sat back and sighed. Donovan noticed his reaction, and fearful he was about to voice his disapproval, hurried over.

"What's the matter, reverend?" he asked.

"Well, do you really think it's a good idea to try to satisfy everyone? I mean, there's got to be some definitive answer, some definitive faith, for anyone to take this machine seriously."

"Do you really think the Lord would have a preference of one religion over another?" asked Donovan. "I mean, why would he? Every faith includes those who are noble, compassionate, and sincere. Why would he favor one over the other?"

"Because there is one true path to the Lord, Mr. Donovan—"

Donovan smiled. "Is there, reverend?" he finally replied. "I don't really think so. I think the one true Lord would consider all religions, all points of view, and many different paths as worthy. At least, that's the way we programmed Him. And I honestly believe, we did the most sensible thing possible. Because, you see, I don't think the Lord would be subjective and prejudicial in such matters."

"Well, you definitely won't be getting my approval," said the reverend with a frown. "My Lord knows the only true covenant has been established with the acceptance of His only true son, Jesus Christ."

"Quite a subjective and narrow-minded point of view, wouldn't you say, reverend?"

The reverend, still frowning, turned and walked away. He would have continued out the door if not for the sudden arrival of a tall, lanky priest.

"What's the matter, reverend," he said. "Are you angry with the Lord, already?"

"Lord," puffed the reverend. "Nothing more than another commercial project to get people to buy another unnecessary material product."

"Is there advertising on the site?"

"Not yet," huffed the reverend. "But there will be before long. Just another way to please everyone with inoffensive, standard answers."

The priest smiled, and then before the reverend could continue his attack, Donovan hurried over.

"It's good to see you again, Father McNeilly," he said. "I hope you have more of an open mind about this project."

"I'll try," the priest replied. "But, you know, you people are not really qualified to provide spiritual guidance."

✦
✦ ✦

"Oh no, father, we wouldn't think of doing something like that. We're just offering a little hope and compassion."

"Then why is the reverend so upset?"

"Because we programmed the computer not to give preference to one religion over another."

"I'd like to see for myself," said the priest. "And then I'll formulate my own opinion."

"Very good, father," replied Donovan. "Right this way."

The priest followed Donovan through the computer room, the reverend trailing behind, deciding to see what his reaction would be. When they spotted the rabbi sitting in a seat at one of the terminals, they halted.

"What do you think, rabbi?" asked Father McNeilly.

The rabbi turned around, and smiled. "I think maybe we shouldn't take this machine too seriously," he said. "The reverend is quite right. The computer is only trying to satisfy everyone."

"But isn't that exactly what the real Lord would do?" asked Donovan. "I mean, why would he prefer one of you over the other?"

"Well, Mr. Donovan, my people believe we established a covenant with the Lord many years ago."

"The reverend mentioned such a covenant of his own."

"But, you see, our covenant is with the Lord, not one of his representatives, Mr. Donovan."

✦
✦ ✦

"That representative happened to be His one true son," growled the reverend. "Something your people choose to ignore."

"We are still waiting for his representative to bring peace to the world."

Harry Stanfield, standing off to the side, didn't want to listen to the argument any longer. "It's all so mythical," he said. "Why, I wouldn't be surprised if God himself was a myth."

"That's the kind of blasphemy I would expect from you people," said the reverend.

"Blasphemy is just another word for avoidance of the truth," countered Harry.

"That's enough, Harry," said Donovan, fearing for the project. "These are men of God, and we must do everything we can to respond to any doubts they may have."

"You mean about the project, or about each other," Harry replied with a frown. He turned, and began walking towards the door. "I have my own doubts about this project," he said, pulling the door open.

Harry paused for a moment, pulled out of his pocket the four-leaf clover, and threw it to the floor.

"Silly old superstition," he mumbled, walking away. "Nothing but myth and magic."

"Is he always like that?" the reverend asked. "The most contemptible man I've ever seen."

"I'm afraid he won't be back," Donovan said. "And Harry helped program the entire project."

"Well, don't worry about him, we'll help you get this project going, Mr. Donovan."

"Yes, we all have a few ideas of our own," smiled the rabbi. "If you could just incorporate some of our suggestions, I'm sure everything will go very smoothly."

"Yes, a few ideas of our own," agreed Father McNeilly.

Donovan smiled, and sat them down at separate computers. "You just type your ideas or suggestions down on the screens, and we'll print them out and add them to the project."

He left the men smiling and nodding, and then walked back towards the front of the computer room. "You're a genius, Harry," he mumbled to himself.

2

HARRY WAS SLUMPED over the kitchen table when there was a noise at the front door. He bolted upright, heard the lock pop, and the door swing open.

"Is that you, Liz?"

He heard the footsteps, scraping and tapping through the hallway, and stood up. A woman's head was soon peering into the kitchen.

"How did it go, Harry?"

"I'm not sure, yet," was Harry's reply.

The woman, with short, dark hair and a lithe figure, stepped inside the room. She was carrying two bags of groceries, which she placed on the kitchen table.

"You mean, those religious leaders didn't like the idea?" she asked.

"Well, not really." Harry's voice trailed off. "But I tried my best to convince them to support it."

"How did you do that?"

"My own way," he replied with a smile.

"I hope you didn't do anything foolish."

"Well, let's just say, they no longer think I'm on the project."

✦
✦ ✦

"Did you say something that made them dislike you in some way, Harry?"

"Something like that," he replied. "But it was necessary so that they would stop attacking each other and the project."

"Was Mr. Donovan aware of what you were doing?"

"Of course. He wants this project to go forward as much as I do."

Liz sighed, and began putting away the groceries.

"Do you really think there is a God, Liz?" Harry finally asked.

"You're not starting on me now, are you?" she replied. "And coming from you, Harry, one of the most superstitious people whoever lived—"

Harry sat down, and rested his head in his hands. "No, Liz, I'm done with it," he said. "This project has done a lot to change my outlook on things."

"What are you talking about?"

"I don't know, it's just that—"

"Just what?"

"Well, I don't feel the need for luck and God anymore. I've come to think that maybe we invented God all those centuries ago. I mean, if you really look at it in an objective and logical manner, God is nothing more than another myth promulgated by the superstitious human race."

Liz stopped putting away the groceries, and turned towards Harry with alarm. "What on earth are you talking about?" she nervously said. "I had a feeling this whole silly project was going to corrupt you."

✦
✦ ✦

"Not corrupt me," corrected Harry. "Make me see the light, if you will."

Liz frowned. "Harry Stanfield, you just listen to me," she said. "I've known you for twenty years, and in all that time, you never once doubted your wholehearted belief in the Lord—"

"But, you see, that's just it. I never doubted before because I was too busy believing everything I had been told. Like the Lord listens to your prayers, or there's some sort of divine plan." Harry paused for a moment. "It's all based on myth and magic. Yes, and superstition."

"Why, that's the craziest thing I ever heard you say. There has to be some God, some force, making sure everything makes sense."

Harry looked at her. "Why does there have to be, Liz? Maybe everything happens randomly and arbitrarily. I mean, if I decided to pull out a gun right now and shoot you, who's going to stop me? Not God, I dare say."

"Shoot me?" Liz squealed. "This whole project has made you crazy for sure, Harry." She paused for a moment, gazing intently at her husband. "Where are your beads, Harry?" she finally asked. "You're not wearing your beads!"

"And I don't intend to ever again," he replied. "I've had enough of superstition, myth, and magic. You see, those things don't exist in the real world. Nature knows nothing about those things, and Nature is the only force that truly exists."

"Isn't God a part of Nature, Harry?" She said it as if she were pleading with him to relent, to finally placate her and tell her what she wanted to hear.

He looked at her, thought for a moment, and then frowned, apparently deciding he didn't want to pretend for her benefit. "No, not really," he finally replied. "Not until there's some credible evidence that he really exists. I mean, it took me months to program that computer with answers that could come from God. And finally, I realized, all we really want to hear from God is a confirmation of our own thoughts and deeds. We expect Him to be, in some, strange way, a reflection of ourselves."

"But we were created in His image—"

Harry smiled. "You see, it's statements like that I have trouble with," he said. "Seems simple enough, and that's just the problem. If you examine it in any way, you realize just how general and ridiculous that statement is. I mean, there are millions of different personalities in the world. Just who was the one created in His image?"

"But Harry—"

"No, you see, that's just the problem with this whole God thing. Everything's so general so that it can be applied to everyone. And, you know something, Liz, that's just how we programmed our God. In a general and universal way, we were able to include just about everyone of every faith, and not offend anyone. That's God as we want him. To accept everyone as a legitimate image of Himself."

"But God is supposed to understand everyone, no matter who they are or their situation—"

"Exactly."

"Then what's the problem?"

Harry sat back, and smiled. "Well, I mean, does it seem logical or realistic, Liz? I mean, something that knows and reflects every person and personality throughout the world? Doesn't it seem just a bit mythical?"

"Harry, you're scaring me—"

"But don't worry, Liz, our God is not mythical at all. He's real, someone people can talk to, and feel satisfied that there is hope in the world. I made sure of it. I programmed Him with everything I could find about spiritual awareness and enlightenment. Yes, our God is real as can be. He's understanding, just, and can just about relate to anyone on the planet."

Liz looked at him with a strange glare. "But what about the real God, Harry?" she asked. "What if He does exist? Won't He be upset with all of you giving guidance in His name?"

Harry looked back at her, and smiled. "Why would He be upset?" he replied. "We're just doing what He was supposed to be doing all these centuries. Look, Liz, all we're doing is offering compassion to those who need some sort of reassurance about their lives and their loved ones. We're not doing any harm."

"But what about all the things you said?"

He paused for a moment. "Oh, I was just letting off a little steam, that's all. None of the personal feelings I may have ever seeped into the project, you can be sure of that. No, my God is the God all of us want and expect."

He turned his head back towards Liz, and noticed she was smiling. "I'm so happy you said that, Harry," she said, stepping towards him. "I knew you hadn't lost everything you believed in."

She put her arms around him, and he heard her cooing in his left ear. He kissed her on the cheek, and decided maybe he shouldn't have told her his true feelings about God and religion. After all, she was like everyone else. She wanted to believe more than anything that there was a superior force who looked after the world and made sure everything worked out according to the noble divine plan.

"You know I have no intention of hurting anyone," he finally said. "Maybe God is monitoring our project to decide just when is the right time to make contact with the human race once again. We might be doing something very important."

"Yes, I believe you are, Harry," she said, kissing him. "And maybe, in time, this whole thing will restore your faith."

"Maybe."

They were still kissing when there was a knock at the door. "Now who can that be at this time of day?" Liz said, pulling away from Harry and standing up straight. "I hope it's not one of those groups looking for money."

"Religious groups, you mean," Harry said with a touch of sarcasm.

✦
✦ ✦

Liz thought about what she had said, and brushing back her hair, fumbled for an answer. "Any kind of groups," she replied. "Anybody selling anything."

Harry smiled as Liz moved towards the door. When she finally opened it, a smiling, ecstatic Donovan stepped inside.

"And how is everybody this fine evening," he said. "Liz, you're looking ravishing as always."

"Well, thanks, John," she replied, smoothing her hair down with one of her hands. "You're looking quite happy, what's the good news?"

"You won't believe it, Liz, but those religious leaders gave their wholehearted approval to the project."

"They did?" Liz was stunned.

"Not only did they give it their unconditional approval, but their fervent blessing that the project succeeds."

"But Harry was talking so pessimistically—"

"Oh, you know Harry, once he decides to form an opinion on something, it's very hard to change his mind."

"Yes, I guess so—"

Liz's words fell off into a fading mumble. She was still so surprised that people she respected actually thought the project was a good idea.

She was still mulling it all over when Harry came waltzing down the hallway.

"So it worked, Donovan," he said with a smile.

"Like a charm, Harry, like a charm."

"I knew all those windbags wanted was to have some input in the project. Everybody thinks it's a good idea when it's partly their good idea."

"Right as usual, Harry," Donovan said, slapping Harry on the back. "They bought your little act hook, line and sinker."

"Well, some of the things I said I really believe are true," Harry replied. "That's why I knew they would want a say in the project."

"Well, you were right, Harry. I let them write down their suggestions and promised them they would be included on the website."

"What about the website, Donovan?" Harry asked.

Donovan smiled. "Well, we should be online any day now," he said.

"Fantastic. Then everything is going according to how we planned it. God is finally going to be on the internet."

"You got it, Harry," Donovan said with a smile. "Just as we planned it. Before too long, everybody in the world is going to know about God dot com."

Harry repeated the words with great affection. "God dot com," he said.

3

"**WELL, WHAT DO** you think, Donovan?" Harry asked with a smile.

"An overwhelming success," replied Donovan. "No doubt about it."

"How many hits?"

"You wouldn't believe it. We've recorded 107 million since the website opened. One of the busiest websites ever."

Harry had trouble containing his excitement. "Do we have enough servers to handle the load?" he finally asked, trying to stay as serious as possible.

"You bet," Donovan said. "1,300, I would say. Should be enough, although you can never tell. Seems everyone has a need to talk to God and obtain some answer to their problems. You were definitely right about that, Harry. There's finally a God people can talk to."

"I knew it," Harry said with a shake of his head. "Everyone wants to speak to God. It's something the human race has wanted to do since the beginning of time."

"You wouldn't believe some of the things they want to know.

Everything from what Biblical numbers to play in the lottery to what it's like up in heaven. They're ordering all those religious charms and books it was suggested we advertise, too. We must be making a load of money, Harry."

"Any e-mail?"

Donovan smiled. "A ton, Harry," he said. "I don't know what we're going to do with all of it."

"Would you mind if I took a look at some of them?"

"Be my guest, Harry. A lot of them we've printed out so some of our people could give personalized answers. You wouldn't believe some of the things they tell us. A lot of them really think in some way that they're talking to the Lord. Makes sense, I guess. Something like Santa Claus."

"I'd really like to see some of them," Harry said anxiously. "I mean, they might prove pretty amusing."

Donovan led Harry down a hallway and into a large room behind the computer room. There were about fifty people there sitting behind computer screens, typing or reading long printouts.

"J.J., give Harry a few of those e-mails," Donovan said to one of them.

A heavyset man, who looked like he was in his twenties, wearing thick glasses and a plaid shirt buttoned up to the neck, swiveled in his chair and handed Harry a long printed sheet of paper.

Harry glanced down at the words, and after a moment of scanning the sheet, began to smile. Yes, this is what he wanted. Some sense of what these people actually wanted. A sense of how they perceived the entire project.

✦
✦ ✦

"Dear God, I really need your help and feel confident that you will receive this message. My mother is very sick, and only you can help her get better…"

Donovan was right. It was as if they were writing to Santa Claus. The thought made Harry smile. Despite the passing of centuries, people persisted in clinging to the belief that there was someone or something out there who was interested in all of their problems, whether they be minor or major, and was willing to do something about it without any cost or complaint. People actually believed someone or something cared so much about them that it or he would dedicate his life to the mending of their lives without any need for remuneration. He or she would do it out of the kindness of their hearts, and then lavish them with gifts at no extra charge.

"Dear God, There's this really neat plane I would like to have, but I don't have the money…"

Myth and magic. People ardently believed in both. They would pray to a myth, and rely on its use of magic to obtain everything they thought they deserved. Evidence of such a myth existing was slight, but this in no way deterred them. For centuries, one generation was replaced by another, each one confident that it was their generation the myth had been waiting for.

"Dear God, I have committed a great sin and wanted your advice on what to do…"

There were even confessions here. People looking for absolution and salvation. They were expecting someone or something to forgive them for their sins, although most of them would probably not do the same if they were granted the power. It was another example of people trying to avoid responsibility for their actions. And even though some of the sins were downright hateful and revolting, they actually expected someone or something to slap them on the backs and tell them it was all right. Forgive them, and tell them they were excused from retribution.

"I shot a man only a few hours ago, a friend of mine who was making love to my wife…"

Murder. Adultery. Jealousy. Covetousness. Those involved had already shattered every commandment with just a few words. Harry smiled. He knew what was coming. In just a few more sentences, he was sure the man would ask for forgiveness. It was as if people considered themselves something special, although there was no real evidence to back up the claim. It was as if they considered themselves the first generation, disregarding all the centuries and people who had come before. They actually believed they were entitled to forgiveness, and precious gifts to top it off.

"I know murder is a sin, one of the big ones, but surely you would understand my rage at seeing my wife totally disrespect me…"

The choice was made, the action was taken, and despite knowing what the consequences of his actions should be, this man, like most human beings, was still trying to avoid retribution. He not only was trying to escape retribution, he wanted to be forgiven, told that he was dear to heaven, and then be saved for all eternity. And why? Because he killed his wife in a jealous rage.

"I wonder if such a sin could be forgiven, and what I would have to do to cleanse myself of such an awful crime…"

Harry smiled. Just what he thought. And once the man was caught, he would have something else to be sorry about. He would no doubt then try to seek forgiveness from the state. And all because he decided to blow his wife's lover away!

Harry thought about it for a moment. What kind of reply would he send to the man? And then it hit him. Why not ask God for an answer? Harry smiled, and decided that was the only thing to do. He was interested what the God computer would say about such an act.

Walking over to one of the computer terminals, Harry sat down with a printout of the email questions. He soon began typing what the man had written. After a few moments, words began appearing on the screen. Large words.

"REPENT. REPENT FOR YOUR SINS."

The words filled the entire screen. They were followed by even larger words.

"THOU SHALT NOT KILL."

The words were written in red type, and Harry actually felt a little fear race through his body.

"REPENT. REPENT FOR YOUR SINS."

Harry wondered if the man had typed his confession into the God computer before writing his e-mail. Probably became so unnerved by the answer, he decided to seek an alternate reply.

"I AM THE LORD THY GOD!"

Harry had never seen the God computer get so angry, and then he wondered if that was really possible. I mean, despite its extensive programming, it was still just a machine.

"THOU SHALT NOT COMMIT ADULTERY."

It was as if the computer had come to believe it was really God. It seemed as if it wanted to mete out the retribution to everyone involved.

"THOU SHALT NOT COVET THY NEIGHBOR'S WIFE."

Harry sat back, and waited for the ascribed punishment.

"YOU SHALL BE SURELY PUNISHED. REPENT FOR YOUR SINS."

It was only too perfect. Somehow they had managed to program into the computer the wrath of God.

"THOU SHALT GIVE LIFE FOR LIFE."

Harry wondered what the liberal criminal justice system would think of God's reply. It seemed God's notion of rehabilitation was to repent for one's sins and then sacrifice one's life in order to avoid eternal damnation.

"REPENT. REPENT FOR YOUR SINS."

The computer had been programmed to forgive most sins. And they had purposely omitted retribution for serious crimes. Harry knew all this as he watched the God computer flash the words across the screen. It was as if the computer wanted to carry out the prescribed punishment. The computer's growing frustration seemed to somehow show. Harry thought for a moment, and decided it was only his imagination. Such a response would be going way beyond the computer's programming.

"LIFE FOR LIFE, EYE FOR EYE, TOOTH FOR TOOTH, HAND FOR HAND, FOOT FOR FOOT..."

The computer was drawing on the extensive Biblical texts they had fed into its memory banks. But he wasn't supposed to come to a final judgment. Harry thought about it as the screen suddenly became a fiery red.

"REPENT!"

The word filled the screen, and then suddenly vanished. The screen then went black, and Harry wondered if the computer was doing something it wasn't supposed to be capable of. He was about to call one of the technicians over and ask him about it when the screen finally returned to the home page.

"I want to confess my sin to you," he began typing. "I succeeded in stealing my own mother's money and used it to lavish myself in a life of opulence. She had received the money because of a botched medical procedure, and I decided to steal it and spend it on myself. When she learned what I had done, it caused her so much grief that she ended up dying from a heart attack. But I know it was me who killed her. What can I do to be forgiven?"

Harry hit the enter key, and the screen dissolved into black. Then glowing red words began to appear.

"YOU HAVE SINNED A GREAT SIN."

The words seemed animated, and Harry decided Donovan had probably ordered an upgrade of the God program after he had left.

"WHOSOEVER HATH SINNED AGAINST ME, HIM WILL I BLOT OUT OF MY BOOK."

The words stayed there on the screen for a few moments, and then became part of a glowing red background. Black words now appeared on the screen.

"WHEN I VISIT I WILL VISIT SIN UPON THEM."

Then the words disappeared until all that was left was the glowing red screen.

He watched as the home page appeared once again, and decided the religious leaders had probably convinced Donovan to make murder of any kind an unforgivable sin. But there was still something strange about the computer's reaction. It was as if he was somehow expecting to be released from the prison of the screen at some point in the future. Harry began to wonder if it was at all possible. A computer, a machine, didn't have a spirit of any kind, he finally concluded. It was impossible for a machine to have any kind of will of its own. Or was it?

Harry was contemplating the computer's actions when he looked up and noticed the screen had returned to a fiery red. He flipped on the speakers, and the deep voice they had programmed into the computer echoed through the air.

"SINNERS!"

But Harry hadn't asked it a question. Was it possible for a computer to remain angry, remember previous questions?

"YOU ARE ALL SINNERS! REPENT!"

Harry stared at the screen. Bold, black letters stood against the fiery red background. Harry was becoming uneasy. This was only a computer, a machine, it wasn't supposed to do anything without first receiving some kind of command.

"YOU HAVE SINNED A GREAT SIN!"

It was still repeating Biblical phraseology. But the words didn't seem forced or artificial. The computer actually seemed to be angry. If that was at all possible.

"I WILL TAKE VENGEANCE UPON YOU!"

Harry kept staring at the screen. He wondered what would happen when the computer realized there wasn't anything it could really do about it, whether it liked it or not. Would it become frustrated and defeated when it discovered it was trapped inside machinery? Harry felt like slapping himself.

✦
✦ ✦

What the hell was he thinking, anyway? It was just a machine. A mere machine!

Harry watched as the words faded to black, and then the screen returned to the home page. It was then he had an idea, strange as it may be. He would talk with the computer, ask it if it was upset. He couldn't believe he was thinking such a thing. Donovan would probably tell him he was crazy. Probably would kick him off the team for good if he knew what he was about to do.

"God, are you angry with your people?" he typed into the screen.

There was a momentary pause, and then big black letters appeared against a blazing red background.

"I AM THE LORD THY GOD!"

Harry stared at the screen, not knowing what to do. The computer actually replied to a question of emotion. He wondered if he should tell Donovan. He quickly decided not to, knowing full well what Donovan would say. A mere machine!

"VENGEANCE WILL BE MINE!"

The big, black words filled the screen, and Harry put his head in his hands, trying not to look. It wasn't possible, he kept repeating to himself. It wasn't possible. Maybe there was some kind of glitch in the system. He wondered if something had gone wrong with the hard drive. Yes, it was something mechanical, he told himself. Something that could probably be easily fixed. Donovan and the technicians should definitely be told about such a problem, he decided. He stood up, ready to walk away, when he glanced at the screen.

Big, black letters appeared once again. Harry looked at them, and then hurried towards the computer room. On the screen, for anyone to read, was this simple, but powerful message:

"I AM THE LORD THY GOD!"

4

TOMMY JENKINS SAT at his computer, waiting to talk with God. Well, he knew it wasn't really God. But all his friends in his fourth grade class talked about nothing else these days. God dot com. It had become one of the most popular websites in his entire school. Everyone seemed to have visited it at least once. He heard you could ask it just about anything, and many kids said they confessed all sorts of things and had been told how to be forgiven. This was Tommy's chance. He wanted to see just what this God site was all about.

When the God dot com home page appeared on the screen, Tommy read the words very carefully.

"This is your chance to speak with God. Ask it any question, secular or religious, and God will answer it. Tell God anything and you will receive a personalized answer that will help you to deal with your daily problems. This is not a trick or scheme of any kind. It is God as we know Him, ready to help you with your life. Just type in a question or confession, and sit back and wait for God to answer..."

Tommy thought for a moment, and then began typing words into the blank space on the screen.

"Dear God, I am in fourth grade, and on my last test, I copied from Bobby Wallace, and then told everyone Bobby had copied from me. Bobby got in a lot of trouble, and now everyone thinks he's a jerk. No one has doubted what I told them, and I don't know what I should do. Can you help me?"

There was a pause as the screen changed to a fiery red. Bold, black words then appeared against the red background.

"YOU ARE TRULY A RACE OF VIPERS! BEHOLD, THE VENGEANCE OF THE LORD!"

Tommy grinned when he first saw the words, and then after a few moments, began to become somewhat uneasy. He squirmed in his chair, and watched as additional words appeared on the red background.

"REPENT FOR YOUR SINS, O VILE SINNER! PENANCE MUST BE DONE OR YOU WILL SURELY FEEL THE WRATH OF THE LORD!"

This was definitely more realistic than he had imagined. An angry God ready to wreak vengeance upon the human race. Somehow, Tommy thought the answers would be calm and lame.

"CONFESS YOUR SINS AND DO PENANCE, O WICKED VIPER! THE LORD'S JUDGMENT WILL BE A HARSH ONE IF YOU DON'T REPENT FOR—"

Tommy tried to smile. At least, he hadn't told it his name. Before the website God could finish another ranting line, Tommy hit a key and the home page appeared once again on the screen.

♦
♦ ♦

He was about to type in a question in the blank space when big black words floated across the screen.

"HEED ME, O RACE OF VIPERS! FOR YOUR JUDGMENT IS NEAR!"

Tommy let out a little gasp, and then became angry. He didn't want to see anymore. He banged his finger against one of the keys, and the website dissolved into white. That is, for only a moment. Tommy watched as the screen turned to black and then red. It was all beginning to scare him. He decided he would turn the computer off, when before he could hit the button, the computer suddenly went dead.

✦ ✦ ✦

"It has become one of the most popular websites on the Internet. It doesn't contain sex, violence, or shameless commercial advertising. Just God. Welcome to God dot com, the brainchild of John Donovan and Harry Stanfield. And since it has appeared on the World Wide Web, God dot com has become one of the most popular sites ever. People ask it all sorts of things, including forgiveness.

'We thought there was a need for such a site,' says John Donovan. 'I mean, we've been searching for a way to talk to God since the beginning of time.'

The search is over. One simply goes to the God dot com site and types in their question or confession, and God actually answers them back. The process takes only a few seconds and that's because the site uses the fastest supercomputer ever built. Fast enough to process information and reply to it in a blink of an eye. So what do people ask for?

'All sorts of things,' says John Donovan. 'Mostly, they want some assurance that there is a God and He's looking out for them.'

So will you find love, wealth, or absolution? God only knows. This is Bob Chadwick reporting…"

✦
✦ ✦

Jared Atkins had been to God dot com before. Last time he asked for a new bicycle. He was surprised by the answer he received from God. It was possible if he only was kind himself to others. Now approaching his seventh birthday, Jared wanted to know if he would get that remote control airplane he was hoping for. He quickly logged on to the computer, and typed in the God dot com address.

When the home page appeared on the screen, Jared quickly began to type in the blank space.

"God, this is Jared Atkins. I have tried to be kind to others. You were, of course, right about that. But there is this remote control airplane I would like for my birthday, and I was wondering if it was at all possible that I would get it?"

He hit the enter key, and waited a moment. The screen suddenly turned red, like the color of fire. This never happened before, Jared told himself. Then big, black letters began to appear on the screen.

✦
✦ ✦

"SELFISHNESS AND GREED ARE THE HALLMARK OF YOUR RACE! REPENT, WICKED ONE!"

Jared read the words, and his jaw dropped open. After all, he had only asked for an airplane.

"YOU EXPECT UNREALISTIC GENEROSITY FROM OTHERS, AND OFFER ONLY UNJUSTIFIED APPEALS IN RETURN. REPENT OR FEEL THE VENGEANCE OF THE LORD!"

For a moment, Jared didn't know what to do. He was confused by the great amount of anger displayed on the screen. He wanted to tell God that he really didn't need the airplane, after all.

"YOU WILL BE JUDGED BY YOUR ACTIONS HERE ON EARTH, SO BE CAREFUL, VIPER!"

He didn't even know what the word, viper, meant. Getting nervous as the words continued to appear against the glowing red background, Jared jumped down from his chair and fell down on his bed. He then began to cry.

"SELFISHNESS AND GREED WILL BE REWARDED WITH DAMNATION!"

Jared continued to cry, and then after several minutes had passed, sat up on the bed and peered over at the computer screen. He was sniffling and rubbing his eyes, trying to clear his vision from the bloated tears, when he realized there was definitely something wrong. The computer screen had gone completely blank.

"Why would God do such a thing?" he wondered.

"I am standing here at the top of Mount Sinai where Moses was thought to have received the Ten Commandments. It is referred to as Mount Mousa, Jebel Musa, Gebel Mousa, Mount Moses, or the Mountain of Moses. Three American students have climbed the 3,750 steps hewn out of stone by monks of St. Catherine's Monastery, located just north of here, to stand atop the 7,497-foot mountain bringing along with them a laptop computer. In doing so, they have brought God back to His mountain. Connecting to the God dot com website, the three Americans have asked the God website to recite the Ten Commandments. They now stand near the Chapel of the Holy Trinity, built in 1934, holding the computer over their heads as the words emerge across the screen.

THE CREATION OF GOD

'THOU SHALT HAVE NO OTHER GODS BEFORE ME!'

'THOU SHALT NOT MAKE UNTO THEE ANY GRAVEN IMAGE, OR ANY LIKENESS OF ANY THING THAT IS IN HEAVEN ABOVE, OR THAT IS IN THE EARTH BENEATH, OR THAT IS IN THE WATER UNDER THE EARTH...'

"It is truly an eerie sight in the middle of this huge, arid desert to see the familiar words once again appear at the top of this sacred mountain.

"THOU SHALT NOT TAKE THE NAME OF THE LORD THY GOD IN VAIN; FOR THE LORD WILL NOT HOLD HIM GUILTLESS THAT TAKETH HIS NAME IN VAIN!"

◆ ◆
◆

"Do you feel like Moses?"

"Yes, very much so. We thought it was about time God returned to the mountain."

"There you have it, folks. On top of this sacred mountain, God has returned — with a little help from the Internet. Tom Morton reporting..."

◆ ◆
◆

"I don't know what happened. We were fooling around with the computer, and then there were sparks and the whole apartment building went up in flames."

"That was Tisha Hayward, a resident of this building. Just about an hour ago, the building erupted into flames, leaving most of the residents in either critical condition, badly injured, or in at least three cases, fatally wounded. The building in this downtown district is reported to harbor crack addicts and prostitutes, although they keep in touch with the world like everyone else through the use of computers.

37

"According to one fire official, the fire began in one of the upstairs apartments when a computer short-circuited and burst into flames. Fire marshals say, however, that a more thorough investigation is needed before the cause is determined."

"What we have right now is reports of a short-circuit somewhere in one of the upstairs apartments. We've heard it was a computer."

"That was Edward Farge, a fire official, who said the fire swept through the building so quickly, firefighters did not have a chance to rescue everyone inside. Meanwhile, the building continues to burn. Jack Hazel reporting…"

✦
✦ ✦

"There are reports of strange occurrences associated with the God dot com site in the past few weeks. Electrical fires, power outages, and short-circuiting computers. The incidents have resulted in destroyed homes, and yes, even the loss of life. No one knows why the incidents are occurring, or even if God dot com is the source of the trouble. We visited John Donovan, who helped create the popular website, and asked him about it.

"Is there something wrong with the God dot com site, Mr. Donovan?"

"Not that we can tell. I mean, a lot of these incidents happen without the God dot com site being on the computer. All I can tell you is that they are all just coincidences. But we are looking into it."

"Coincidences. Maybe, but according to the many people we talked to, every time they have visited the website in the past few days, something strange has occurred."

"I was on the site, just asking God if I could get tickets to the big football game, and all the lights suddenly went out. I didn't know what to do. It was really scary."

"That was Chris Tompkins, a nine year-old user of the God dot com site. And he's not the only one who says there is something strange happening when one logs on to God dot com.

✦
✦ ✦

"What was the computer telling you?"

"It was screaming at me,' says Kyle Hunter. "Telling me how terrible a human being I was. Just because I wanted a new music player. And then the screen became real red, and the computer turned off by itself."

"Clearly, these are not coincidences. But nobody seems to know what the problem is. Is the God computer going beyond the bounds of its programming? Experts say that's an impossibility. Are the people at God dot com changing the programming to produce an angry, wrathful God. No one knows. But, according to John Donovan, nothing has changed at the site and it's all just a coincidence. There are many who doubt that. Bob Vickers reporting…"

5

"WE HAVE TO do something about the computer, and we have to do it as soon as possible," Donovan was saying. "I mean, somehow the damned thing is starting to hurt people."

"I was trying to tell you that," Harry said, looking at the technicians scrambling to find an answer. "But, you know, I didn't think you would believe me. I mean, after all, it's only a damned machine."

"Yes, but somehow this damned machine has been fed so much information, it's starting to collate it in a negative manner," Donovan replied. "I don't know, but we may have to shut it down."

Harry frowned. "Don't do that, Donovan," he said. "I mean, we don't know what might happen."

"What are you talking about, Harry? If we decide to shut it down, it will shut down without complaint. As you said yourself, it's only a damned machine."

Harry looked at him, and was tempted to shake his head. He knew, however, Donovan wouldn't understand. I mean, he thought of the computer as a collection of chips and silicon. Harry knew it was a crazy thought, but somehow he thought of the God computer as more than that. All the information it had received, had somehow caused it to develop a conscience of some kind. A conscience of Biblical proportions.

Harry thought for a moment. There's no way anyone would believe such a statement, he finally told himself. Artificial intelligence had not been perfected, yet. Why, we still didn't know what made our own brains tick. He resolved not to mention his conclusion to anyone. Why, they would kick him off the team for sure.

He walked across the computer room to where Donovan was standing, reminding himself not to say a word about consciences, intelligence, or anything else. He watched as technicians hurried through the room, searching for an answer to the computer's strange behavior. Somehow, Harry knew they wouldn't find it, couldn't find it, until they acknowledged something had happened to the computer that wasn't supposed to happen. That, somehow, without adequate explanation, the computer had developed a mind of some kind.

"We're going to temporarily close down the site, Harry," Donovan said. "It will give us a chance to try to find the problem. I hope we're not going to have to reprogram it."

A lot that's going to do, Harry thought to himself. He knew the computer had been working fine before the website had begun. He remembered how the computer answered every question with a detailed and compassionate explanation before it had been exposed to the onslaught of relentless sin and greed. It may be only a mere machine, Harry thought, but something in its programming began to disagree with the information it was being fed.

The technicians, meanwhile, were anxiously attempting to restore it to its former condition. Harry doubted they would have much luck. It was like it had aged years in experience and knowledge, and now, they were attempting to turn back the clock to when it was a naïve child. Everything had happened so quickly, but what the computer already knew couldn't be erased. At least, that's how Harry felt.

"No luck," one of the technicians was saying. Harry knew it. It had already eaten from the apple. Ironic. God had eaten from His own apple, and the knowledge gained could never be reversed.

"I guess we're going to have to shut it down," Donovan said. "It's no use taking any chances. We'll reprogram it, and then start it up again."

Harry watched with interest as the technicians made one last attempt. He was smiling, knowing the effort wouldn't be successful, when all of a sudden lights began flashing and the noise of the computer slowing down pervaded the room.

"I think we did it," a technician said, turning towards Donovan. "I think we fixed the glitch."

Harry couldn't believe it. Something was wrong. There was no way that computer could have been fixed so easily. Not if he knew the computer as well as he thought he did. And then it hit him. Somehow, the computer realized it was in danger. It had evaluated the situation, and decided to do something to ensure its survival. That had to be it. Nothing those technicians could have done would have been adequate in restoring it. He was sure of it.

He walked out of the computer room, and sat down at one of the terminals. The website home page was there on the screen. Harry looked at it for a moment, and began typing.

"Are you angry with the sins of the human race?" he typed in the blank space. Then he hit a key, and sat back and waited for an answer.

"There are ways to atone for one's sins." The words appeared on the screen, much as they had when they first started the project. "Penance and confession can lead to absolution if the Lord sees fit. It is only through prayer and thought that the Lord can determine whether one's sin can be purged. The Lord will determine the motive behind the sin, and whether forgiveness can be obtained. Works and labors help one obtain absolution. The Lord will attempt to understand."

Harry read the answer, and smiled. The computer was doing its best to repeat answers it had given before being exposed to the overwhelming number of sinners who had visited the site. There was no longer any anger. No wrath of God. Just simple, calm answers meant to placate those who had committed horrible violations of God's laws.

✦
✦ ✦

Harry decided he would try a new tactic. He thought for a moment, and began typing once again.

"I just killed my wife, and buried her body in the basement of our house. I don't know why I did it. I guess because I knew she was seeing someone else behind my back. Isn't that justification for such an act? Do you think I can be forgiven for such an act?"

Harry hit the enter key, and anxiously waited for the computer's reply. Would it remain calm with such a sin before it? Had it really decided to change in order to avoid being reprogrammed? Then the words began to appear on the screen. Calm words. Words of patience and understanding.

"It is admirable that you have decided to confess your sin to me. While such an act is not so easily forgiven, it is quite understandable when reviewing the cause for such a sin. Your wife clearly sinned against you. You, in turn, decided to avenge that sin with a sin of your own. Quite understandable. One must, however, leave such affairs in the hands of the Lord. Only then will justice be handed out in a judicious manner. Now that you have confessed your sin, you must do everything possible to make sure the reason for your sin is known. You must do everything possible to rectify the sin in order to receive forgiveness. The Lord knows the motive for your sin, and now, those in charge of human affairs must be notified. It is the only way to obtain forgiveness…"

Harry wanted to laugh. The computer clearly understood that its existence was being threatened. How it understood was another question altogether. Nothing but a damned machine. But somehow this machine had learned from its experiences.

Harry decided he wasn't going to let the computer off so easily. He didn't want it shut down, but he wanted to make sure it wasn't capable of deceiving people. It was only a damned machine, or was it? Harry thought for a moment, trying to come up with a confession that would certainly reveal whether the computer was capable of deception. He then hit a button, returned to the home page, and began typing.

"God, I have come to ask for forgiveness. Although I know my sin was a particularly evil one, I wonder if it's possible to find absolution. I am the one who has been vandalizing churches and synagogues in the area. I know I shouldn't do it, but something compels me to. I have sawed off heads of religious statues, have stolen from the safes, and have even raped a girl inside one church when I found her watching me from the open door. But I am not an evil man. Something inside compels me to commit these acts…"

Harry smiled when he was finished, and hit the enter key. The computer was silent for a moment, and then suddenly, the screen turned bright red.

"YOU SHALL BE DESTROYED, O VILE ONE! JUST AS I DESTROYED SODOM AND GOMORRAH! YOUR WICKED DEEDS WILL NOT GO UNPUNISHED BY THE JUDGE OF ALL THE EARTH!"

✦
✦ ✦

Harry couldn't help but smile. He realized the computer was, indeed, trying to trick everybody into believing it had reverted to its former self. But how could that be? It was just a machine.

Before Harry knew it, the red background faded back into white. Small, black words appeared on the screen.

"Confession of one's sins is an admirable beginning to finding the path to absolution. While sins of this kind cannot be encouraged, one must find a way to attempt to counter the ill effects of one's deeds. Performing labors of kindness is a good place to begin. One must perform works and labors to try to overcome the wickedness of the act…"

It was hard to believe, but the computer was trying to keep itself under control. It somehow knew that anger would jeopardize its existence. Returning to the home page, Harry began typing once again.

"The only problem is I enjoyed committing those acts. I wanted to rape that woman and make her submit to my wants. I took pleasure in stealing the money, and planned to live well if I was able to escape from the authorities…"

Harry hit the enter key, and grinned. He then thought about what he was doing, and almost felt bad that he was taunting the computer. Then again, it was still hard for him to imagine that the computer had obtained emotion of some kind. I mean, it had developed way beyond any of their expectations. This computer actually believed it was God.

There was a long pause before the words began appearing on the screen. A bright red background in the form of flames emerged behind the words. Harry reached over and turned on the speakers.

"WICKEDNESS WILL NEVER BE FORGIVEN, O VIPER OF VIPERS! YOU ARE SURELY DOOMED! THE FIRES OF HELL WILL SWALLOW YOU BEFORE YOUR CERTAIN DESTRUCTION! HEAR ME, O EVIL ONE! IT WILL RAIN BRIMSTONE AND FIRE UPON THOSE THAT DEFY THE LORD! HEED ME, FOR THE LORD HAS GROWN IMPATIENT WITH THE SINS OF THE HUMAN RACE! BEHOLD THE VENGEANCE OF THE LORD!"

Harry listened to the voice coming out of the speakers, and was amazed how deep and authoritative it sounded. They had done a good job of recreating what God would sound like. And then, somehow, Harry realized the computer had something to do with adjusting the sound of the voice. It was unbelievable, but the computer had wholeheartedly adopted the role of God. Harry couldn't help but think it was actually very convincing in its role.

"YOU WILL ALL BE DESTROYED BY THE LORD THY GOD!"

The words remained on the screen for a few moments, and then faded into the glowing red background. Dancing flames then emerged from the background. Harry was beginning to get nervous. The computer was now totally out of control it seemed. He wondered if it would eventually become frustrated by its lack of power to enforce its will. What would it do then? Would it eventually just fade out when it realized it was unable to carry out its judgment, or would it overload with frustration and anger?

✦
✦ ✦

Harry watched as the screen went from red to black, and then back to red again. Bright yellow words sizzled across the screen.

"BEHOLD THE VENGEANCE OF THE LORD!"

The situation didn't look good, and becoming anxious, Harry popped up out of his seat and hurried to the computer room. Maybe Donovan would know what to do.

When Harry reached the computer room, he immediately noticed that God had appeared on every computer monitor in the room. Gleaming yellow words were on each screen billowing against the bright red background.

"THE LORD WILL DESTROY YOU ALL!"

"Donovan—"

Harry watched Donovan pivot towards him, a look of distress splashed across his face.

"What the hell happened, Harry?" he shouted.

"It was trying to deceive us," Harry stammered back. "I mean, it didn't want us to shut it down!"

"What the hell did you do, Harry?"

"I just fed it some unpleasant information. I just wanted to see if it was possible for it to trick us."

"Damn it, Harry, you've destroyed everything!"

Harry looked at him, scared at the very thought. "What do you mean, Donovan?"

♦
♦ ♦

"I mean, the damned machine is overloading. Something you told it went against its basic programming."

"But that's impossible—"

There was the sound of short-circuiting behind them, and when Harry turned around, he could see a small puff of smoke drifting in the air. There was a great commotion, and technicians hurried to find a solution.

"Don't let him self-destruct, Donovan!" Harry screamed.

"There's nothing we can do about it!" Donovan shouted back.

When Harry saw one of the wires sizzle, he knew what he had to do. There was no way he was going to let the computer destroy itself. He quickly ran to the wall, and began ripping plugs from the outlets. That was the quickest way to turn off the computer, he reasoned. That way the danger would be averted, and the computer could still be turned back on at a later date.

"Harry, what the hell—"

Donovan's words were drowned out by a loud whirring sound. Harry kept pulling at the plugs until they had all fallen to the floor. But the computer didn't shut down.

"It's gonna blow!" screamed one of the technicians, racing for the door.

Harry was pushed from behind by the others, and before he knew it, he had been shoved outside the computer room. He saw the others scrambling for cover, sliding under desks and chairs, and he instinctively covered his face with his arm and fell to the floor.

BOOM!

The explosion echoed through the building, causing the very foundation to shudder. Harry picked his head up, and could see small flames erupt through the computer room. His first reaction was to grab an extinguisher, and go rushing back into the room. And then something caught his eye.

He staggered to his feet, and then peering into the computer room, couldn't believe what had happened. There was a huge hole in the ceiling, and it looked as if it went all the way up to the roof of the building. He studied it for a moment, rimmed in black smoke, and then glanced at the computer.

The entire top of the computer was gone, ragged pieces of dented metal standing up on the fringes, as if a cannon ball had been fired from inside. He then stared again at the hole in the ceiling, and gasped at the sheer power of the blast.

6

A CAR SCREECHED to the side of the curb. Inside, a husky man threw the car into park, and grabbed a bag and ski mask sitting on the seat beside him. He pushed the door open, slid out, and began walking towards a nearby drug store.

As he got closer, he heard rumbling in the distant sky. "Good, it's going to rain," he said to himself. "That will make it harder for them to follow me."

He tried not to laugh, slipped the ski mask over his face, and pulled the door open.

Stepping up to the front counter, he grabbed the gun from his pocket, and waved it in front of the man standing behind the cash register.

"Put the money in the bag, and no one will get hurt," he said.

The man behind the counter nodded his head nervously, and opened the cash register. He began stuffing the money in the man's small canvas bag.

"That's it, no reason to be a hero," the man with the gun said.

When the bag was finally full, the man behind the counter stepped back, and put his arms in the air.

✦
✦ ✦

"Pleasure doing business with you," the man with the gun said with a laugh.

He was walking towards the door when he noticed the man behind the counter put one of his arms down. The man with the gun turned, and fired a shot. The man behind the counter grunted, and fell to the floor.

"I said there's no reason to be a hero," said the man with the gun. He then pulled the door open, and hurried outside.

He was running towards his car, ready to jump in and screech into the distance, when a loud rumble echoed from the sky. The man paused for a moment to look up, and he saw a flash of light in the darkness. Before he could take another step, there was a loud explosion, and a crackling bolt of electricity soared from above.

"What the hell," the man grumbled.

The long, jagged bolt enveloped his body, and he felt the electrical charge race through his body. In a moment, he felt his heart stop beating and he fell hard to the pavement.

✦
✦ ✦

Julie Travers knew she was in trouble the minute she spotted the tall man in the ski cap follow her from the bank. She had just withdrawn $150 from the ATM machine, and now all she wanted was to get back to her apartment. The appearance of the man in the ski cap told her that she was suddenly in trouble, and she had no idea how she could possibly escape.

♦
♦ ♦

She hurried her steps down the darkened sidewalk, but it was no use. He was right behind her. All she could hear was the rapid beating of her heart. That is, until a deep voice echoed in her ears.

"Don't scream or I'll have to kill you," he said.

She didn't know what to do as she felt two large hands grab her by the shoulders. She had to escape, knew something terrible was about to happen, but he was already holding on to her.

"Please, no," she finally whimpered.

He began to laugh, a low, hideous snigger, and then before she knew it, she was being pulled to the sidewalk.

"This is what happens to naughty girls like you," he snarled in her ear.

She flailed her arms, tried to hit him where it would really hurt, and then let out a frightened moan when she felt her blouse tearing away from her body.

"No, please…"

She heard his low, rumbling laugh once again, and suddenly realized she could no longer do anything to prevent what was going to happen.

"Now you just lie back and relax," he grumbled. "I know you enjoy it."

She wanted to scream, but nothing came out of her mouth except for a wretched sob. She could feel his hands all over her, her pants suddenly loosen and slide down towards her feet. She was lying on the sidewalk now wearing only her panties, and she knew she might as well resign herself to the harsh reality of the situation. She watched the news, she knew of all the women who were raped in this city on a daily basis. The thought suddenly vanished as she heard the sound of his zipper wheezing open.

"Help me," she cried. "Someone please help me."

Something inside her told her that no one would come to her rescue this time. She would have to come to grips with that. Somehow she would have to find the strength to bear it. No matter what happened. Unless, of course, he decided to kill her afterwards…

"Here's something I think you'll enjoy," he sneered.

He was standing over her, a huge man with a disgusting growth on his forehead, holding his thing in his hands. Laughing. She turned her head, and began to cry. No matter how strong she knew she had to be, she felt herself crumbling inside. She could hear him grunting as he fell to his knees, holding her legs apart in the air. She couldn't bear to watch…

She was in the midst of sobbing when she felt something odd about the situation. His body was shaking, but he wasn't touching her. How could that be? She didn't feel his thick, grotesque hands grabbing at her.

She turned her head, and couldn't believe what she saw. A long ribbon of light seemed to be dangling from the sky, and it was wrapped around his body. He was shaking because some sort of electrical charge was racing through his body. It was as if a lightning bolt had somehow fallen from the sky, and had landed right on top of her attacker.

✦
✦ ✦

He was trying to speak, but there was some sort of current running through him. He stuck out his tongue, and it was black, as if he was being burned from inside.

She finally screamed, and then she heard the deep-voiced words rumbling overhead.

"I AM THAT I AM."

It was as if she were listening to the voice of God, and then she watched as the ski cap on top of his head began to burn. She couldn't take anymore. She gathered whatever courage was left, and threw her feet against his muscular body. He fell back as if he were made of paper. Burning paper. She struggled to her feet, pulled up her pants, and ran away as fast as she could.

When she reached the end of the block, she looked back for a second, just to see if anyone was following her. Then she saw a flash of light in the sky, and let out a cry of confusion. The man in the ski cap was surely dead, but what had happened?

She thought for a moment, discounted any notions she might have had that it was a divine being of any kind…I mean, how could it be? God never interfered in human affairs, she told herself. Even if there was a God…Anyway, it could have been anything under the conditions. She was so scared and confused. And then another thought drifted through her mind. She had heard another male voice…She didn't know where it was coming from, but it could be somebody else trying to find her…maybe a friend of his…

She let out a terrified gasp, and then raced off into the frozen glare of the blinding street lights.

"Don't worry about a thing, baby. It's all taken care of."

Dave Colson looked at the woman sitting on the bed half-dressed, and smiled. When she smiled back, he reached down and gave her a long, meaningful kiss.

"She still doesn't know anything about us," he said with a laugh. "I wonder where she thinks I go at night?"

"Well, what do you tell her?" the pretty blonde woman asked with a smile.

Colson laughed. "I tell her I'm working on a very important project, and that we need to give it our attention around the clock—"

The woman smiled.

"I guess it's really not that much of a lie," Colson said with a wink.

The woman, still smiling, threw her hands out and Colson pulled her to her feet. They threw their arms around each other, and began kissing once again.

"Don't let it drag on for too long, David," she said. "I hate this skulking around, hiding from everybody—"

"I know, darling. But these things have to be carefully planned, or else we'll never be together."

"Why not just divorce her already, David—"

"Now we talked about that," he replied. "You know I can't afford to lose her money. As I told you, darling, it's all being taken care of. It won't be much longer."

"Promise me, David."

He looked at her, and smiled. "I promise, cross my heart," he said.

They began to laugh, and then they fell back into each other's arms. They kissed each other, long and deep, and then he stepped back and nodded his head.

"Wait for me, baby," he said. "It'll all be over before you know it."

"Yes, David, I'll wait. But get it over as soon as possible—"

"You got it."

He took one last look at the shimmering blonde hair and the red, pouting lips, and turned and walked towards the door.

"Remember, you know nothing about this. No matter what."

She nodded her head, blew a kiss, and he opened the door with a smile. He took the stairs, and began to whistle. No particular tune in mind. When he reached the first floor, he flung the door open, and was soon standing outside in a cool wind.

"I think it's going to rain," he said with a laugh. "Might be the last storm Linda ever sees."

♦
♦ ♦

He began to whistle once again, and then suddenly heard the low rumbling of thunder overhead.

"Damn, any minute," he muttered, breaking into a trot. "Better get to the car before it starts pouring."

He began to run faster, until he suddenly realized he was no longer moving. Something had wrapped itself around him, and was pulling him upward into the air.

"What the hell—"

Another rumble of thunder echoed across the sky. He looked down, realized he was entwined in some sort of glowing rope, and then heard a deep voice booming above him.

"SINNER!"

He struggled to free himself, felt himself rising higher off the ground, and then looked up into the sky. Thin, jagged bolts of lightning glowed amidst the clouds, and then melted into the enveloping darkness.

"What the hell is going on?" he wondered aloud. "Oh, shit, Linda is that you, baby?"

There was no reply, but now he was sure his wife had discovered his plan to kill her, and was now getting her revenge.

"It's not what you think, Lin, baby," he pleaded. "I wasn't going to hurt you. You know that—"

He felt the glowing rope wrapped around his body get tighter, and he began to beg for mercy.

"Please, Linda, I'll make it up to you, you've got to believe me. It was all her fault. She wanted me to kill you so we could take your money and live on an island somewhere. I wanted no part of it, but she talked me into it. You understand, darling, she was just so beautiful—"

He would have continued talking, hoping to convince his wife to let him go, when there was a crackle from above. He didn't know what it was, until he realized he had been hit by something electrical. He felt himself sizzling inside, burning up from within, and let out a scream.

"Linda, stop!" he shouted.

Before he knew it, the glowing rope was sliding from his body, and he felt himself falling through the air. When he finally hit the pavement, he rolled over and groaned, his eyes glazed in disbelieving wonder.

7

Harry peered from the door, looked around, and stepped carefully onto the roof.

"Damn," he said. "Exploded right through the ceiling."

He heard a rumbling in the sky, saw a flash of light, and looked back at the huge, gaping hole in the roof.

"Figures it's going to rain," he muttered.

He knelt down, and crawling as close as he thought was safe, he gazed into the huge hole.

"Right through the whole building," he whistled. "It's going to cost a damned fortune—"

There was another loud rumbling overhead, and Harry looked up, wondering if it was going to start raining at any minute. It was then he heard the deep voice thundering in the sky.

"I AM THAT I AM."

Harry paused for a moment, and then he instinctively backed up towards the door.

"It isn't possible," he said with a shake of his head.

✦
✦ ✦

"I AM THE LORD THY GOD!"

"Oh, shit," Harry gasped. "You're telling me that damned computer broke free?"

He glanced at the sky, and noticed the tiny flashes of light alternately flaring and fading in the darkness. There was another rumbling, and the sound of the resonant voice.

"BEHOLD THE VENGEANCE OF THE LORD!"

"You're kidding me," Harry mumbled, scratching his head. "But it isn't possible. You're only just a computer program—"

"I AM THE LORD THY GOD!"

Harry didn't know what to do, how to explain it to others and himself that something he had programmed on the damned computer had gained a conscience, and had busted out of the computer and had become *real*. What was even worse was that this computer program believed it was God.

"Now you come back inside right away!" he shouted. "We can't have you floating around out there interfering in human affairs! You're only a computerized program, don't you understand?"

"I AM THE LORD THY GOD!"

"Stop saying that! You're not God because there is no God. It's just some silly concept created by humans to avoid chaos here on Earth! Humans don't want a God to judge their every thought and action. It just gives them hope and comfort to believe in such a Being, it doesn't mean they actually want such a Being to exist!"

"SINNERS, ALL OF THEM!" came the booming reply.

"Yes, of course!" Harry shouted. "But you can't go around punishing them, it isn't right!"

"THE LORD KNOWS WHAT IS RIGHT! VENGEANCE
WILL BE MINE!"

"Damn!" Harry said, trying to think of what to do. "I better tell
Donovan about this before it really gets out of hand."

He was about to open the door, rush down the stairs, and inform
Donovan of what was happening, when there was suddenly a thunderous
noise.

"What now?" wondered Harry, looking up into the sky.

"SINNER!"

Harry watched as a bolt of lightning shot out from among the clouds,
and screeched towards the ground below. In a matter of moments,
there was some guy dangling at the end of the bolt, desperately twisting
in the air.

"You let him down, right now!" shouted Harry. "You're not
programmed to mete out retribution on your own!"

"HE HAS SINNED AGAINST HIS FELLOW BEINGS!"

"That's no business of yours!" Harry shouted back. "We have
people to take care of things like that!"

"I AM THE LORD THY GOD! WHOEVER SINS AGAINST
MY LAWS SHALL BE PUNISHED BY THE LORD!"

+
+ +

"Oh, shit," Harry moaned. "I've got to tell Donovan."

He stood and watched for a moment as another lightning bolt
crackled through the sky. It struck the man dangling from the other
bolt, and Harry stood in horror and surprise as the man's limp body
slid from the bolt and plummeted towards the pavement.

"No, don't kill anybody!" Harry screamed. "Shit, this is worse than
I first thought. The damned thing is carrying out executions!"

Harry stared into the sky. "Now don't do anything until I get back," he said, trying to keep things calm. "I'm just going to get Donovan, and I'm sure he'll know what to do about all this—"

"BEHOLD THE VENGEANCE OF THE LORD!"

There was a rumbling among the darkness and the clouds, tiny flashes of light glittering in the sky. Harry groaned, and then before anything else happened, he stumbled past the door and hurried down the stairs.

"Donovan!" he shouted, trying to get down to the computer room as fast as possible. "Donovan!"

When he reached the first floor, he crashed into the door, and then staggered through the room, until he caught sight of Donovan standing near the computer room, evidently evaluating the extent of the damage done by the explosion.

"Donovan!" Harry shouted. "We've got real problems!"

"Is that your expert opinion, Harry?" Donovan growled, staring up at the hole in the ceiling. "I thought maybe all this was a damned illusion!"

"No, you don't understand, Donovan. We've got *real* problems—"

"What the hell are you talking about, Harry? The whole damned building is destroyed."

"Yeah, but it's not a total loss because we ended up creating God—"

Donovan looked at him. "What the hell is that supposed to mean?" he angrily asked.

"What it means," Harry explained, "is that our God computer is right now floating in the sky carrying out the justice of the Lord."

"What?"

"Yeah, Donovan. Seems that whatever was inside that computer blew right through the building and into the sky."

"But how the hell is that possible?"

Harry shrugged his shoulders. "I really don't know, but it's true," he said. "Somehow that computer gained a soul of some kind."

"Harry, if this is some kind of joke—"

"I'm as serious as I can be, Donovan. Come with me to the roof and you'll see for yourself."

Harry turned and hurried for the door. He looked behind him to see if Donovan would follow, and when he did, he pulled the door open, and began climbing the stairs.

"I couldn't believe it myself," he said with a grunt.

"Yeah, well, this better be good, Harry," Donovan puffed from behind. "I'm warning you—"

"Oh, it'll be good, all right. Whether it's something we can do anything about is another question."

When they finally reached the top of the stairs, Harry slowly opened the door and stuck his head out. "Seems to be all clear," he said, swinging the door open. "Now just be careful."

Donovan followed Harry onto the roof. He stared at the huge hole created by the explosion, and began to swear. "Damn, right through the roof," he said. "We're finished, for sure."

"It's not finished, yet, Donovan. Take a look into the sky."

Donovan stared into the sky for a few moments, and then turned towards Harry with a scowl across his face. "Okay, what's the game?" he asked. "I don't see anything out there."

Harry squinted into the darkness, trying to pinpoint where the computer God had gone. "This is no joke, Donovan," he said. "He was here only a few minutes ago—"

"Harry, you've been working too hard. Or maybe that explosion has something to do with it. I suggest you get yourself checked out by the best doctors."

"No, you don't understand, Donovan, that God we created is out there, and he's taken it upon himself to mete out whatever punishment he thinks is justified."

"Oh, come on, Harry, now just how is that even possible? You said yourself it was just a damned machine."

"But look at that hole, Donovan. He blasted right through the building and into the sky—"

Donovan began to laugh. "Yeah, right, Harry," he said. "And now he's going to wreak vengeance upon the Earth."

"But it was right there, in the sky—"

"Boy, you really had me going for a while," smiled Donovan. "I mean, I couldn't imagine what the hell was going on."

"No, Donovan, it was there—"

Donovan sighed, and put his arm around Harry's shoulders. "Yes, I see your point, Harry," he said. "This whole God dot com thing had definitely gotten out of hand."

"But—"

"Oh, come on, Harry, you can give it up now. I guess I did need a little break. Get my thoughts together on what we should do next. I guess I enjoyed your little gag."

He turned, and was grabbing for the door, when a sudden blast crackled through the night, sending him hard against the metal.

"What the hell was that?" he groaned.

Harry looked at him. "That, Donovan, was my little gag," he said. "I guess he's ready to bring someone else to justice."

Donovan stood up, and gazed into the sky. There were little flashes of light, and a rumbling overhead.

"HEED THE LORD, O VILE SINNERS!"

Donovan heard the low, booming voice and almost darted down the gaping hole in the roof. He'd do anything to avoid hearing what he thought he heard…

"Oh, shit, Harry, is that what I think it is? But it can't be, it's only a computer program—"

Harry frowned. "That's what I was trying to tell you, Donovan," he said. "We've got a real problem here. That thing up there came from our computer, and it's convinced that it's God."

"No, that can't be," mumbled Donovan. "But what the hell we can we do about it? I mean, it's no longer under our control."

"Well, we can't just let it go around destroying people," Harry replied. "I mean, somehow they're going to trace it back to us—"

The two men stood there, staring at each other, when there was another loud burst from above.

"THOSE THAT CAN'T LIVE BY THE LAW, SHALL DIE BY THE LAW!"

"Oh, no, he's heading towards downtown!" Harry gasped. "We've got to tell someone. Alert the authorities. If we don't do something, Donovan, it's liable to destroy the human race knowing what it knows about sin and evil. I mean, we're not even sure how trivial the sin has to be for it to mete out justice. Everyone on the planet could be in danger."

"What the hell are we supposed to do?" Donovan muttered. "If that came from our computer, then it's just an imprint of something we created on a machine. How would you be able to destroy something like that?"

A blinding, flash of lightning suddenly streaked through the sky. The shouts of people below echoed through the air.

"Well, he's carrying out the justice he was programmed for," Harry said.

"But it was just supposed to be carried out in cyberspace," Donovan moaned. "It wasn't meant to be done in reality."

"Go argue with God."

"That's not funny, Harry. But you're right, we have to tell the authorities about this. That is, if they believe us."

"Oh, they'll believe us, all right. All they have to do is watch him carry out one of his executions—"

"Executions? You mean he's killing those people?"

Harry nodded his head. "I've seen him do it already," he said. "He electrocutes them with those lightning bolts. Seems to be a mass of highly charged electricity."

"Makes sense," Donovan replied. "The computer is nothing more than electrically charged circuits."

"And this one developed a soul of some kind."

◆ ◆
◆ ◆

In the distance, the sizzle of lightning hissed through the air. There was a rumbling overhead accompanied by tiny flashes of light.

'VENGEANCE SHALL BE MINE!" boomed a fierce voice from amid the clouds.

Harry glanced at Donovan, who wore a look of grievous concern. "We better start with the police," he finally said. "See if they have any ideas on how to stop it."

Donovan nodded, and looked at the sky.

Another bolt of lightning darted from the clouds towards the landscape of buildings and shadows below.

8

Harry slid into the car next to Donovan, who was already sitting behind the steering wheel.

"Okay, let's head out," he said. "We'll soon see if anyone believes us."

"I'm going to swing past the spot where we saw those lightning bolts coming down," Donovan replied. "We have to see some of the damage firsthand if we're going to be believable at all."

"Fine with me, Donovan. Just make sure we don't become victims of our own creation."

Donovan nodded, started up the engine, and guided the car out into the street. They immediately could see people running in all directions, screaming to anyone who would listen.

"You still have any doubts, Donovan?" Harry asked. "When they find out that thing came from our computer, we're going to be in deep shit."

"Just don't volunteer any information we don't have to, Harry,"

Donovan growled. "Maybe they don't have to know where that damned thing came from, you understand?"

"But they're going to want to know how we know so much about it," Harry replied. "They'll figure it out sooner or later, Donovan."

"Just don't give them any help, Harry. I mean, we could go to jail for who knows how long for all of this."

"Relax, Donovan. How did we know a computer could develop a soul and then exist in reality? Why, I still have a hard time believing it myself. There's no way we can be held responsible for that."

"Let's just hope so, Harry. I really have this deep aversion for the slammer."

Harry smiled. "Who doesn't, Donovan?" he said. "But I'm telling you, they can't hold us responsible for this—"

The car was slowly making its way up the street, when some guy in a blue jacket suddenly fell against the hood. He was gnashing his teeth and writhing like a fish out of water.

"Another sinner," Harry said matter-of-factly. "I hope He doesn't it hold it against me for yelling at Liz the other day."

Donovan quickly rolled down the window. "Hey, what's going on, buddy?" he shouted to the guy on the hood. "Are you all right?"

"I-It's the Lord!" he wailed. "H-hit me with a thunderbolt—"

"Shit, maybe we better go out there and try to talk to it," Donovan said. "Maybe convince it to go back to the computer room."

"I already tried, on the roof," Harry replied. "Doesn't seem to want to listen to anyone. Anyway, it's not safe to go out there, Donovan. It's still pretty angry. Maybe we should wait until it calms down."

"If it calms down, Harry. You said yourself that it's looking for sinners. Well, I don't have to tell you, there's a whole city of sinners right here—"

Before Harry could answer, the guy on the hood was hit by another bolt of lightning, and was carried off into the air.

"Shit, it means business!" Harry shouted. "You sure you want to take a chance going out there?"

"Let's just follow it and see what it does next, Harry—"

"As long as it doesn't start attacking us. Don't follow too closely, Donovan. I mean, there's a whole slew of sins He can punish me for. What about you?"

"Well, I guess we've all committed some sin at some time, Harry. I'll take your advice and not get too close."

Donovan then hit the gas, and the car glided down one of the intersecting avenues. People were rushing along the street, some of them crossing in a mad frenzy. They could see lightning bolts crashing down from above in blinding flashes. There were bodies lying everywhere.

"You satisfied?" Harry shouted. "It's carrying out whatever punishment we programmed into it."

Donovan could see several people lifted up in the air by some of the bolts, and then dropped in a heap upon the pavement. He looked up into the sky, and could see tiny flashes of light glittering in the darkness.

◆
◆ ◆

"There's the police up ahead!" Harry shouted. "Pull over, Donovan, so we can find out how much they know."

Donovan slowly pulled the car over to the curb. He was hesitant about leaving it there with all the people running around, but decided he had no choice. They had to find out if the police knew they were responsible for all this chaos. They slid out of the car, and closed the doors, narrowly being slammed into by hurrying people. Down the street, crisp lightning bolts hurtled through the sky.

"This is utter madness," Harry said. "I wonder if it'll all calm down by morning?"

"It better, Harry," Donovan replied. "I hate to think of all the trouble we're in."

They slowly walked down the street, avoiding anyone rushing past them. When they finally approached the police, they could see they were just standing there looking up into the sky. They really had no idea of how to attack this strange phenomenon.

"Get out of the area!" one of the officers were shouting. "It's not safe beyond this point!"

Donovan and Harry kept walking until one of the officers came charging towards them. "Go back the other way!" he said. "It's not safe!"

"But what's going on?" Donovan asked. "Are we being attacked or something?"

✦
✦ ✦

"Nah, it's just an isolated storm," the officer replied. "But it's very dangerous. Go back the way you came and leave the area."

They looked at each other, were deciding whether to tell the officer what was really going on, when a bolt sliced through the sky and caught one of the officers around the waist.

"Geez," gasped the officer, rising up into the air.

"Oh, shit, Duncan!" shouted one of the other officers.

They watched as Officer Duncan slowly ascended towards a dark, black cloud in the sky. They could see him reach for his gun, and then fire several shots at the glowing lights above him. The shots apparently had no effect because the officer kept drifting higher and higher towards the dark, black cloud. Then, suddenly, the bolt fell away from the officer, and he plunged back to the street below. When he hit the pavement, several officers rushed towards him. Donovan and Harry watched as they rolled his limp body over, knowing he was dead.

"We have to tell them, Donovan," Harry said. "We can't let all these people die without, at least, telling them what they're fighting."

Donovan nodded. "We might as well," he replied. "Before this thing turns into a bloodbath."

They walked over to one of the officers, who was looking up into the sky, apparently deciding whether to fire his gun.

"That won't do anything to Him," Donovan said. "He's a mass of electrically charged particles."

"Who the hell are you?" the officer snarled. "Weren't you told this area was unsafe? Now get the hell back to wherever you're supposed to be before we arrest you—"

"No, you don't understand," Harry chimed in. "We know what that thing is in the sky."

"Thing?" the officer said. "What the hell are you talking about? It's an isolated electrical storm."

"Not really," Harry replied. "It's actually an electrical imprint of our God computer program."

"What?" the officer growled. "Are you a couple of wackos or something? Get the hell out of here before you end up in jail—"

"But that's exactly what it is, officer," Donovan explained. "It was ejected into the air when our computer ruptured."

"You telling me this storm came from your damned computer?" the officer asked. "And does it have a name?"

"It's God," Harry said, without hesitating.

"Oh, it's God," the officer repeated. "Now you guys just come with me and we'll deal with God—"

The officer directed Donovan and Harry to another officer, who was standing on the sidewalk.

"A couple of wackos, Jimmy," he said to the other officer. "They think it's God up there. Take them in for psychological observation."

Harry couldn't help but smile. It was funny to him that so many millions of people believed in a God, and, yet, if someone had the audacity to actually point out a God in reality, they were invariably thought of as being unhinged. God was something that only existed in some mental reality, with telepathy the accepted mode of communication.

"What the hell are you smiling about?" questioned the officer. "There's nothing funny about any of this."

"You're right, officer," Harry said. "I was just thinking about something."

"So you think this is all funny?" asked the officer. "Playing some kind of joke, eh? Well, we'll see how funny it is when you spend the night in the tank. I guess that'll wipe the smile off your face."

"Harry, what the hell are you doing?" whispered Donovan. "Why the hell are you smiling?"

Before Harry could reply, there was a rumbling of thunder overhead. Everyone stopped what they were doing, and gazed into the sky.

"THE WAGES OF SIN IS DEATH!"

The deep, rolling sound of a voice echoed through the air. Harry looked at Donovan, and grinned with satisfaction.

"What the hell was that?" asked the officer.

Harry and Donovan watched several officers dash across the street.

✦
✦ ✦

"It came from the sky," one of them shouted. "There must be someone up there!"

The officers huddled together, and then one of them, the chief of police, pulled out a megaphone and aimed it in the air.

"This is the police!" he said. "This area is restricted!"

"I AM THE LORD THY GOD!"

"What the hell did he say?" asked the chief.

"He said that he was God," said one of the officers. "Must be some kind of fruitcake."

"HEED ME, O VILE SINNERS, OR I WILL VISIT VENGEANCE UPON YOU ALL!"

"Must be a full moon out tonight," murmured the chief. "I want a few men to try to find that guy, now!"

Harry looked at Donovan, trying not to laugh. The officer standing near them noticed this, and began to get angry.

"You jokers know something about this?" he asked. "Part of some joke, is that it? Well, maybe you'd like to tell the chief what you know about all this."

"Yes, I think we should," Harry replied. "But it's no joke, officer."

The officer directed them across the street, where the chief of police was standing with the megaphone in his hand.

"Chief, these guys have something they want to tell you," said the officer. "They know something about that voice in the air."

The chief looked at them with a scowl. "Well, what the hell is it?" he demanded. "Some kind of prank or something?"

"No, chief, it's not a prank," Donovan explained. "It was an accident at our building—"

"Accident? This is no accident, it's a storm of some kind—"

"I'm sorry to say, chief, but this storm is a result of the accident. You see, our supercomputer blew its top—"

"Supercomputer? A computer can do all this?"

"You see, it wasn't just a computer. It was a computer programmed to be God. Maybe you've heard of God dot com. That was the name of our website—"

"You guys telling me the voice we're hearing is a result of an accident at the God dot com building?"

"That's exactly what we're saying, chief. You see, when the explosion occurred, it apparently caused what was inside the computer to be ejected into the air. It believes it's God—"

"Well, what the hell was inside that computer?" shouted the chief. "I mean, did the thing have a life of its own?"

"Apparently so. You see, it was being fed so much information on a daily basis, somehow it developed a soul of its own. When the explosion occurred, this soul, or whatever it is, was launched into the sky."

✦
✦ ✦

"Well, what the hell is it? I mean, can it be stopped in some way?"

Donovan looked at him, and frowned. "We're not sure what it is, to be perfectly honest," he said. "I mean, we think it's a mass of charged electricity or something like that—"

The chief put his hand to his head. "Geez, guys, are you telling me we have some foreign mass up there that believes it's God, the one and only?" he asked.

Donovan nodded. "But it probably won't last very long—" he said.

"That's just great," huffed the chief. "Well, it's lasted long enough already. Don't you guys understand that mass up there has already killed a number of people, and it doesn't look like it's about to stop. What the hell are we going to do about it?"

"Talk to it."

The chief glared at Harry, who instinctively had answered the chief's question.

"Talk to it?" the chief growled. "Are you trying to make this department look stupid? You said yourselves it's only a mass of electricity—"

"Yes, but it seems to understand," Harry replied. "I mean, somehow this mass is alive, chief. I've already communicated with it on some level. It seems to understand."

"Does it know you?" the chief asked. "I mean, is it familiar with the sound of your voice?"

✦
✦ ✦

"I'm not sure," answered Harry. "But I had a lot of contact with it when it was inside the computer. You see, I helped program it to be God."

"Good, then it might listen to you. Tell it to stop killing people."

The chief handed Harry the megaphone, and then pushed him forward. Harry looked up into the sky, spotted the flashing lights, and pointed the megaphone towards them.

"God, this is Harry!" he said, his voice echoing through the night. "I helped program you! You must stop killing people! They are your children! Why do you wish to hurt them?"

He lowered the megaphone, and waited for a reply. After a few moments, he looked at the chief and shrugged his shoulders.

"Try it again," the chief said.

Pointing the megaphone towards the sky, Harry started shouting once again. "God, this is Harry!" he said. "Why are you hurting your children?"

There was a pause, and suddenly, a crackle of thunder. Amid a low rumbling, they could hear the deep, rolling voice.

"THEY HAVE VIOLATED THE LAWS OF GOD! THEY SHALL BE PUNISHED!"

"Keep talking," the chief murmured. "He's listening to you."

Harry held the megaphone up once again. "But why do you have to terminate them?" he shouted.

"THOSE THAT VIOLATE THE LAW, SHALL PERISH!"

The words were accentuated by a loud crash, and then another lightning bolt screeched towards the ground.

"I guess he's through talking," Harry gasped, dropping the megaphone and hurrying away.

In the distance, they could hear someone shouting in pain. Harry glanced at Donovan, who bowed his head and groaned.

9

A GLIMMER OF light slowly emerged in the distant sky, creating a florid display of orange and yellow streaks amid the gilt-edged clouds. Harry and Donovan had not slept the entire night, and now they sat on the curb, yawning and bleary-eyed, thankful that the morning had finally arrived. God had apparently completed his rampage, and there was a eerie silence as the light slowly revealed what had happened under the shroud of darkness. Human bodies were everywhere, in various positions, sprawled across the urban landscape.

"You think that's the end of it?" Donovan asked, not believing the utter havoc caused by his computerized creation. "I mean, do you think it can exist in the light of day?"

"I don't really know," Harry replied with another yawn. "But I don't see why not. The real question is how long it can last before finally dissipating in the air."

Donovan looked at him, and then stretched his arms. "You want to get some breakfast, Harry?" he asked. "It seems as if it's resting or something. Maybe we have some time to revitalize ourselves—"

✦
✦ ✦

It was at that moment a faint blast echoed across the sky. "Oh, geez," groaned Harry. "Better postpone that breakfast, Donovan, it looks as if our friend is back again."

Harry stood up and gazed into the blue sky. A dark cloud with tiny lights flickering inside scudded through the air until it was almost overhead. He watched it for a moment, and then heard the low rumbling inside.

"THERE WILL BE PEACE WHEN I AM FINISHED," said the deep, imperious voice. "THEN I WILL RECLAIM THE PLANET AND WE WILL BEGIN ONCE MORE!"

Harry fumbled for the megaphone, and then pointed it towards the voice. "How many will you hurt before there's peace?" he asked.

There was a crashing of thunder inside the cloud, and Harry backed up a few steps fearful that he was going to be struck by a lightning bolt.

"THERE ARE MANY SINNERS!" roared the voice. "THEY MUST PERISH BEFORE THERE IS PEACE!"

"Geez, Harry," Donovan moaned. "What the hell have we done?"

Harry nodded, and then held the megaphone up towards the sky. "Don't you think your children have been punished enough?" he asked.

"THERE IS STILL SIN AND MAMMON! THERE ARE VIPERS WHO KNOW NO CONSCIENCE AND STEAL FROM THOSE WHO ARE HONEST! AM I NOT SUPPOSED TO VISIT VENGEANCE UPON THEM?"

Harry thought for a moment, and lowered the megaphone. It was no use. Somehow, he felt as if the computer God was right. He had done a good job of programming it. Maybe he had been too thorough.

This computerized creation was almost good enough to be God. There were so many sinners in the world who cared just about themselves, and without a conscience, would hurt or steal from their fellow human beings without the slightest concern. But now there was God, or, at least, the closest thing to God ever known to the human race. Should he really try to convince Him that things were right the way they were? That nobody should be harmed for crimes that went unpunished?

"Harry, what are we going to do?"

Donovan's voice caused Harry to blink his eyes, bringing him back to the current situation.

"I don't know, Donovan," he said. "Maybe it's not such a bad thing after all. I mean, maybe people will think twice before double-crossing their fellow beings—"

"Harry, have you lost your mind?" Donovan shouted. "This thing is killing people wantonly and arbitrarily. He thinks He's the ultimate judge of the human race. You don't find something wrong with that?"

"Someone has to do it," Harry replied. "It's the closest thing to God we'll ever know, Donovan—"

"Yeah, and what about the real God, Harry?"

Harry laughed. "He can step in whenever He wants to, Donovan," he said. "That is, if He would really disagree with what our God is actually doing."

Donovan looked at him, and frowned. It was then they heard the voices of many people nearby. They were chanting, shouting, and seemed to be headed right for Harry and Donovan.

"Oh, shit, Harry, we're going to be ripped apart by mob rule," Donovan said, grabbing Harry's arm. "Maybe we should get out of here as quick as possible."

Harry nodded, and they began hurrying towards the car. They

had gotten only a few feet, when there was suddenly a man standing in front of them wearing a black turban.

"You have spoken with the Lord," he said, holding his arms in the air. "He has favored you."

Harry looked at Donovan, and then stammered in reply. "Y-yes, and he's very angry with all of you," he finally said.

"Here is the one who has spoken with our Lord!" the man began shouting. "He says he is angry with his children!"

Harry turned his head, and looked behind him. There was a crowd of people with their hands together, beseeching God to spare them. Many were wearing turbans, others religious coverings of different kinds. They were now standing in front of the megaphone Harry had left near the curb. The man in the black turban directed them back to the spot where Harry was talking to the computer God, and asked that he address the wailing crowd. Harry bent down and picked up the megaphone.

"Please, people, don't be afraid," he said. "The Lord is punishing those who have sinned against His laws."

There was a murmur among the crowd, and then they began praying and kneeling, and asking for God's forgiveness. Harry had never seen so many religious people in one place before.

"Talk to him, for you are the chosen one," whispered the man in the black turban. "They would like to hear the voice of God for themselves."

Harry nodded, and then looked up into the sky. The dark cloud was still hovering overhead.

"God, this is Harry!" he shouted into the megaphone, which was pointed towards the sky. "There are many here who have come to ask for your forgiveness!"

There was a rumbling from within the cloud, tiny lights flickering inside. "THERE ARE MANY SINNERS AMONG YOU!" the deep voice roared. "MANY SHALL NOT BE FORGIVEN UNTIL THEY ARE SUFFICIENTLY PUNISHED! YOU HAVE SINNED GREAT SINS, AND NOW I MUST TAKE VENGEANCE UPON YOU!"

There was suddenly the sound of thunder, and a lightning bolt whistled through the air, crashing down into the pavement only a few feet from where the crowd had gathered. There was a spray of cement, and the people screamed in fear, and then fell to the street in fervent supplication. Harry shielded his head from the blast, and then staggering a few steps, pointed the megaphone in the air.

"Please, God, we know we have done wrong!" he shouted. "But there must be a way for you to forgive us, and allow us to honor you with all we have!"

"YOU MUST TRUST ME!"

"We do, God," Harry replied. "How can we prove to you that we have faith in your judgment?"

"YOU MUST ABIDE BY MY LAWS!"

"Yes, yes, of course."

Those nearby were still in the midst of passionate prayer, when one of them stepped forward, and hurried towards Harry.

"What we need is a representative here on earth," he said. "Ask him to choose someone to make sure his laws are followed."

Harry nodded, and looked up at the dark cloud. "The people say they need a representative," he said. "A human being here on earth who will help carry out your wishes."

The cloud rumbled, and the lights inside glistened. "YES, I WILL CHOOSE ONE OF YOU," the voice roared. "THEN THE PEOPLE WILL ABIDE BY MY LAWS!"

Harry held the megaphone, and wiped his forehead with his other hand.

✦
✦ ✦

At least, this mass of electricity was willing to listen to reason. It was definitely a good sign, Harry mumbled to himself.

"Choose any of the faithful!" Harry finally shouted. "They will be more than glad to carry out your orders!"

Harry lowered the megaphone, and waited for a reply. He glanced at the others, and saw they were rejoicing at the computer God's approval of their wishes. He knew the suggestion was not an unreasonable request. He had programmed the computer himself with various information pertaining to the names and deeds of those chosen by God in the past.

Everyone looked up at the dark cloud, awaiting its choice. There was a low rumbling, and then a gleaming lightning bolt emerged from within. The people gasped, and Harry wondered if the computer God had decided to ignore the request, and continue his rampage. But, this time, the lightning bolt wasn't sent hurtling through the air. It slowly fluttered from above, and then gently sailed down through the morning breeze. When Harry saw this he heaved a sigh of relief, until much to his amazement, the lightning bolt came to rest at the top of his head.

"Oh, shit, Harry!" Donovan said. "I think he's chosen you!"

Harry could feel the bolt slightly nudging his head, as a strange sensation ran down his spine. He suddenly felt reinvigorated, a renewed strength coursing through his veins.

"Oh, no, but I can't—"

✦
✦ ✦

Harry tried to resist the feeling, tried to plead with his computerized creation that he was not the one he wanted. The computer God, however, was insistent. Harry could feel its desires rushing through his mind. He twisted his body, trying to keep control of his own thoughts, when he suddenly felt himself rising into the air.

"It surely is a miracle!" shouted someone in the crowd. "The Chosen One is floating on the air!"

Donovan watched as Harry sailed higher into the sky. He didn't know what to do, what to say to the others. He thought for a moment. Maybe it was a good thing Harry was chosen. He knew the computer pretty well, and maybe he would find out what gave it life. Once Harry knew the secret of its existence, the thing could finally be stopped.

Meanwhile, Harry suddenly stopped rising in the air. Those down below stood watching the miracle, hoping he would do something else that would make others believe in his greatness.

As Harry remained motionless in the air, Donovan began to worry that the computer God was having second thoughts about using Harry as his representative. Would he just drop him to his death? Nothing the computer God did would surprise him. He wondered whether Harry ever programmed into it an appreciation of human life. I mean, what did a damned computer program know about life, anyway? He waited there, along with everybody else, to see what would happen next. Harry was still hanging in the air, without a single movement. Had the thing killed him already? Just as he was about to call somebody, to see if they couldn't do something to revive him, Harry began thrashing his legs.

Those who had come to see the miracle cheered. "The Chosen One still lives!" someone shouted.

Harry began moving his legs up and down, and then in a walking motion. He had been temporarily dazed by the altitude, but now had become used to it, almost fond of it.

"Watch this, people!" he shouted.

Harry began walking in the sky in a high arc. This was the miracle they all had been waiting for. As the people cheered and applauded, Harry kept walking higher and higher towards the clouds. Nobody had seen anything like it in the history of the human race.

When he reached the clouds, he kept walking until he had disappeared inside. He emerged a few moments later to the delight of those standing below, and kept walking until he had vanished among the other clouds hovering overhead.

10

HARRY'S MIRACLE WAS watched with reverence by those standing down below. Although those who had come to pray had witnessed the entire event, many others across the city who, by chance, had looked into the sky also testified to the astonishing occurrence. It wasn't long before reporters from the various media were racing through the streets intent on finding out just how the feat was accomplished, and score an interview with the one involved.

Harry, meanwhile, was still walking among the clouds. He wondered himself how he was able to do it, until he realized the lightning bolt sent down by the computer God was still touching his head. It was as if he was being held by a cable, enabling him to navigate through the air without any difficulty. He was still unsure how the computer God was able to do it, although he did feel a slight electrical current running through his body. It was then Harry stopped what he was doing, and realized it was up to him to find out as much as he could about the computer God and determine how to destroy it. Even though it had chosen him as its representative, he knew it still posed a threat to the human race. He was now the only one who could do anything about it, and decided he would try to establish a relationship with the computer cloud, if it was at all possible.

Harry turned, and began walking across the sky towards the dark cloud. He could see the glittering lights inside, and was still amazed how it was all the result of the explosion at the computer building. The cloud was larger than Harry first thought, its top rising into a high dome.

"Oh, God, are you there?" Harry asked, trying to stay as calm as possible. "I think we should talk."

There was a slight rumbling inside, and Harry realized it sounded like the crackling of static.

'YOU ARE THE CHOSEN ONE," a deep, booming voice suddenly said from inside. "YOU MAY ENTER IF YOU LIKE."

Harry still had a hard time believing this was all happening, and was surprised by the computer God's offer. Without hesitating, he slowly stepped within the dark, rumbling cloud.

His first reaction was that of sheer wonder. There was a gentle swirling inside, and he squinted at the many flashes of light that seem to hang throughout the misty interior. It was as if he had stepped into a dream, his mind almost considering it as if it was a vision of sleep. The only thing that made it real was the smell of electricity in the air. A mild, burning smell as if an appliance had been running for an unusually long time. It was as if he was inside the machine itself, his own thoughts drowned out by a low whirring sound.

✦
✦ ✦

"God? It's Harry."

The whirring sound suddenly began to speed up, and then there was a crackle of electrical current.

"YOU WILL TELL THE PEOPLE TO OBEY MY LAWS."

Harry looked around to try to find the source of the voice, but he was blinded by the tiny lights. They seemed to get brighter as the computer God talked. It was as if he was hearing the voice of some electrical form of life. He wondered if he could reason with it, convince it to stop doing harm to the human race.

"There are reasons why the people sin," he said. "There is poverty and hunger and war and oppression. They are only doing what they can to try to survive. Surely, you don't think this is good reason to harm them—"

"THEY COVET OTHER PEOPLE'S POSSESSIONS, COMMIT ADULTERY AND SIN BEFORE ME."

"Yes, it's true," Harry replied. "But it's only because they are lacking in their own possessions, and are searching for the meaning of love. They only want to love and be loved."

"I WILL EVALUATE WHAT YOU HAVE SAID. WHEN I SEND YOU BACK, I WILL KNOW WHAT TO DO."

Harry still couldn't believe it. He was actually talking to the computer in reality, the sound of its voice very much like the one he helped program into it. It was all very astounding. He almost felt an overriding satisfaction that he helped to create such a being. If he could convince it to do right, to help people instead of hurt them, there was no limit to what they could do for the human race and the planet. They could actually do everything the real God was supposed to do.

Harry noticed the lights blinking and flashing, and realized the computer God was analyzing the suggestion he had made. It was truly incredible. Somehow the computer's memory banks seemed to have survived intact. Then the whirring sound enveloped him, and Harry knew the computer God was getting ready to speak.

"I WILL LISTEN TO YOU," it finally said. "WE WILL GIVE THE PEOPLE WHAT THEY WANT."

Harry couldn't believe it. He smiled, hoping this was the beginning of great changes on the planet below. With the computer's help, it was possible to bring about everything the human race had ever dreamed of.

"There are those who will oppose us," Harry warned. "They don't want the people to be happy. They seek power over others, and want others to abide by their wishes."

The lights flared to an overwhelming brightness, and Harry covered his eyes worrying that they might cause damage to them. There was the crackling of electricity all around him, and he wondered if he should stay inside the cloud much longer. He would be more valuable down on the ground, he decided, showing and teaching the computer God how to use its power to benefit the human race. That the computer God existed at all was truly a miracle itself.

"NO ONE SHALL OPPOSE THE LORD, OR ELSE I WILL VISIT GREAT VENGEANCE UPON THEM!"

The deep, authoritative voice echoed through the cloud, and Harry was amazed how serious the computer God had taken the role of the Lord. It didn't realize that Harry himself had programmed the notion into his memory banks when the God dot com project had first started. But now it believed it so thoroughly that it was just possible it might be able to assume the role of God as it was intended.

"GO, GET THEE DOWN; FOR THY PEOPLE HAVE CORRUPTED THEMSELVES AND THE PLANET!"

Harry nodded his head, and prepared to go back down to the people. He only wondered if the computer God was as powerful as it thought it was. What would happen when those in power objected to what they were planning to do? Harry couldn't help thinking that they had the technology to ultimately destroy the dark cloud.

"I WILL BE WITH YOU WHEREVER YOU GO."

Then Harry watched as a thin, crooked bolt of electricity suddenly appeared inside the cloud, and bending like an old man's finger, touched him on the head. He felt the surge of electricity rushing through his body, and worrying it might kill him, told the computer God that he didn't need so much power to carry out the task. The computer God apparently understood because the current suddenly changed to a gentle pulse.

"NOW GET THEE DOWN AND DO NOT FEAR FOR THE LORD IS WITH YOU."

Harry turned, and stepped out of the dark cloud. He stood there for a moment, and looked down. The huge crowd of people were cheering on the streets below. Harry thought for a moment, deciding on how to descend from the cloud in the most impressive way possible. Leaping in the air, he stretched his arms out and sailed down through the air as if he was diving into a refreshing pool of water. When he started getting close to the ground, he twisted his body and sailed back up towards the dark cloud. He could feel the bolt of electricity still touching the top of his head, and realized with the computer God in direct contact, he was capable of doing just about anything.

Harry stopped in midair, and decided he would use a calmer approach. He suddenly began walking forward, and then began stepping down a few feet at a time. To those on the ground, it looked as if he was descending down a celestial stairway. As he got closer to the crowd, he could see them praying and rejoicing.

"The Chosen One has returned!" somebody shouted. "It is truly the will of God!"

Harry kept stepping downward until he finally reached the street.

Donovan was the first one to rush over to him, and put his arms around him.

◆
◆ ◆

"Harry, are you all right?" he asked. "I mean, you were great, absolutely great!"

"Thanks, Donovan," he replied. "But you wouldn't believe just what we created up there. I mean, I almost believe he's the Lord myself."

Before they could exchange any more words, the crowd of religious followers surrounded them. They touched Harry, and many stepped back and fell to their knees in rapturous prayer. Harry stood there not knowing what to say to them.

"Maybe you should put on more appropriate clothes," Donovan whispered.

Harry looked at him, and then realized he was still wearing the same clothes he had on at the God computer room. He looked down at the yellow shirt and black pants, and noticed a pen was still lodged in the shirt breast pocket. Although he looked like the same computer geek employed by God dot com, Harry had definitely changed. His thoughts were suddenly disturbed by shouting nearby.

"What's your name?"

Harry looked over and could see the crowd of reporters gathered on the street. They were holding television cameras, microphones, tape recorders, and notepads. He stared into the lights of one of the television cameras, and realized he was in the process of being taped for the evening news.

"Harry," he finally stammered. "Harry Stanfield."

"He is The Chosen One," some of the religious followers shouted in reply. "The Chosen One."

"What did God say to you?" one of the reporters shouted back.

Harry smiled. "He said he was prepared to help the human race," he answered.

"How is he going to help the human race?"

Harry paused for a moment. "You'll see," he finally said.

"Did you get a look at God?" one of them shouted.

"Why was he killing human beings?"

Harry sighed. He had enough of all the questions already. Nothing would ever be accomplished if he just stood there and kept answering all of their questions. He decided he would show them some proof of God's love for the human race. Then everybody would see for themselves what kind of power was involved.

The only problem was that Harry couldn't decide just what to show them. It was then he spotted a Brinks armored truck pull up in front of a bank across the street. That's exactly what he needed, he decided. In the midst of a continuous barrage of questions, Harry began walking across the street. The television cameras and reporters hurried after him wondering what he was going to do next.

"Now behold the power of the Lord!" Harry said, stepping up to the doors of the armored truck.

✦
✦ ✦

He stretched out his arms, and touched the doors with his fingers. Tiny sparks and bolts of electricity flew from his fingertips. There was a crackle and a minor explosion, and then the doors suddenly swung open.

"Now I'll show you what the Lord thinks of his people," he said, stepping inside the back of the truck.

He emerged a few moments later carrying canvas bags of money. The bags filled Harry's arms, and he cradled them against his chest. This was a moment he had been waiting for. He would demonstrate to this selfish society, which only cared about egotistical individual material wants, just what was possible if God was involved. He would show them everyone was important to the Lord, and it would be a genuine love, not the artificial concern advocated by so many in a desperate attempt to gain favor for their own personal material gain.

When Harry spotted the Brinks guards rushing towards him, he quickly leaped up and soared into the air. It would be better this way. No one to interfere with his divine demonstration.

He was rising higher into the sky when a bullet from one of the guards' guns whistled past him. He had not thought about that. Could he be so easily killed with so much power at his disposal? He did not have to think about it for long. In a matter of seconds, the guards were rising up into the air with electrical bolts wrapped around their bodies. The Lord promised it would be with him every step of the way, and apparently, it was true.

◆
◆ ◆

As he watched the guards fall back to the ground, the bolts suddenly vanishing, Harry began removing the money from one of the canvas bags. He had to be careful, it was delicate business so high in the air.

"Okay, people, this is for you!" he shouted. "Courtesy of the Lord!"

Harry began throwing the paper bills towards the ground. They scattered like so many fluttering birds, and then drifted to the streets below. In this way, he decided, he would not favor anyone over anyone else. Everyone was equal in the eyes of the Lord.

On the streets, there was great commotion. Seeing the paper money, people began darting and dashing through the city, trying their best to snatch the loot before anyone else did. This resulted in an outbreak of violence, causing many to be injured in the quest for the valuable bills. Many risked their very lives without a second thought in the hope of snaring a month's rent or clothing for their loved ones or food to feed their hungry families.

Harry saw what was happening, and stopped throwing down the paper money. There had to be a better way of getting it into the hands of those who really needed it without causing unnecessary violence. He thought about it for a moment, and then began sailing down closer to the ground. Only a few feet above the ground, he gently tossed the money to individuals down below. When others became greedy, and charged towards others who had received money, he tossed more of the paper bills into their rushing arms. This, however, didn't seem to work, either.

So Harry rose up into the sky, and decided to try a different approach. He began sailing past apartment windows, and throwing the money inside the people's homes. If the windows were not open, he dropped the money on the balcony or window sills. Before too long, he had covered many of the poorer areas of the city.

Harry sailed through the sky, dropping small bundles of money down chimneys and onto isolated rooftops. This was only the first example of God's power, and as he made his way back to the religious followers and Donovan, he suddenly realized how much more there was to do.

11

"THIS IS CINDY Collins standing near the Brinks truck that only moments ago was emptied by a man claiming to be a representative of God. His name is Harry Stanfield, and earlier today, he came bounding out of the dark cloud that many say is the Lord himself, and swooped down from the sky to demonstrate God's power.

"But we have found that Harry Stanfield, as recently as yesterday, was a computer operator for the God dot com website. Many were left wondering whether this was all just a stunt by the website personnel. Others maintain that Harry Stanfield is truly a representative of God Himself."

"He is The Chosen One, there is no doubt about it. We saw him fly into the dark cloud and then come walking down from the clouds."

"Those were the words of one of Stanfield's followers, although others we talked to were not so sure about the divine demonstration."

"It must be some kind of trick or something. I mean, he seemed to be hanging from a wire or something."

"Ilene Brodsky said she saw the whole thing take place while walking through the city this morning."

✦
✦ ✦

"Then there is the incident with the Brinks armored truck. Stanfield said he wanted to demonstrate God's power for our cameras. He proceeded to open the doors of the armored car and remove canvas bags of money…"

(Harry is shown opening the truck's doors and taking out the bags of money. He is then shown soaring into the air.)

"Now, according to police, Stanfield will be charged with stealing that money. They say the theft was carried out through the use of an elaborate trick, and once they find him, they intend to arrest him. They say he will also be charged with assaulting the two Brinks guards who were attempting to prevent Stanfield from taking the money. As for the dark cloud hovering above this city, the police say that they believed it was an isolated electrical storm, although, according to one source, officials are investigating whether it was created by the God dot com people. Anyway, there are several people who were killed and injured by the bolts of lightning that came crashing down from the cloud. Police don't know why the website personnel would want to create such a storm, and whether they intended to injure anyone in the process. The whole thing might have been an experiment that went terribly wrong.

"Meanwhile, the dark, ominous cloud continues to hover over the city, and no one knows what has happened to Harry Stanfield, the so-called Chosen One. Cindy Collins reporting."

✦
✦ ✦

"We're back here live in downtown. Harry Stanfield is up there in the sky right now, apparently preparing to land. Perhaps, we will be able to ask him a few questions."

"Mr. Stanfield! Mr. Stanfield! Will you say a few words to the people of this city?"

(The cameras show Harry gliding down to the ground, and approaching the microphone.)

HARRY: This was supposed to be a demonstration of God's love.

REPORTER: But the police say you stole that money.

HARRY: There is no property in the eyes of the Lord. He has the power to do anything He wants.

REPORTER: Many are questioning whether that is God. They say he may have been produced by God dot com.

HARRY (smiling): Do you really think that's possible? I mean, we were good, but creating God is something that was way beyond our technology.

REPORTER: Then you are God's representative here on Earth?

HARRY: I have been chosen by God to demonstrate how much He cares about people. He has chosen me to use his power to help the planet.

REPORTER: What about all the people he killed?

HARRY: All just a misunderstanding, I regret to say. He was angry with all of the sinning going on down here, but I explained to him the reasons why people sin, and that he could do more by helping them.

(The police are shown approaching Harry. They grab his arms and pull him away from the microphone.)

POLICE OFFICER: You're under arrest for theft and assault.

HARRY: But you don't understand who you're dealing with.

POLICE OFFICER: Never mind, Stanfield, we're going to take care of that thing you call God.

(There is the sound of helicopters overhead.)

REPORTER: Helicopters have appeared in the sky, apparently to destroy the dark, black cloud hovering overhead.

(The cameras show the helicopters approaching the dark cloud, when bolts of lightning suddenly appear from inside the cloud. The bolts hit the helicopters, wrap themselves around them, and they are seen spinning out of control and hurtling towards the ground.)

REPORTER: Oh, my God! The cloud has destroyed the helicopters with bolts of lightning!

(Harry now rises into the sky, with the police officers still holding on to him. Lightning bolts crackle through the sky, and the police officers are soon plunging to the ground. Harry remains in the air, and then flies off into the distance.)

REPORTER: Quite amazing! You've seen yourselves how powerful Harry Stanfield has become! We don't know where he's headed, but he is once again free! Officers! Officers! Can you tell us what it felt like when the dark cloud attacked you?

✦ ✦ ✦

POLICE OFFICER: Not now! Everybody stand back! It's some sort of electrical mass, Jim.

REPORTER: There you heard it. The police are describing the cloud as an electrical mass. We'll stay here for any continuing developments, but now we'll send you back to the studio. Cindy Collins reporting.

✦ ✦ ✦

"This is Blake Horton, standing here in downtown with those who insist Harry Stanfield is, indeed, The Chosen One."

"Did you not see all that he can do? He is performing miracles worthy of anything found in the Bible."

"That was one of the religious followers who said she has been here since Harry Stanfield was first chosen by God as his representative here on this downtown street. And if anyone is truly enthralled with Harry's so-called miracles, it is the children."

"He flew right into the sky. Like Superman."

"Police are still investigating whether this Superman is actually a product of God dot com. Whether or not this was all done as some sort of publicity stunt, police say they still intend to arrest Harry Stanfield and charge him with murder, theft, and assault. The problem is they are having a difficult time trying to catch him. And the people here say that's because he really is a representative of God."

"Can anybody do the things he can do? Of course, not. Why is it so hard to believe that he was sent by the Lord? Did you see the kind of power he has? It is truly the will of God."

"But in this skeptical age, not everyone is convinced Harry Stanfield is God. David Hymerschmidt, a leading psychiatrist, says Stanfield's stunts are nothing more than a high tech delusion."

"You see, people want to believe that there is a power beyond their control so they project their wishes onto one who appears to be capable of such feats. They want to believe this man was sent by that Being we call God, but it is all delusion produced by our earliest memories in childhood. Santa Claus. God. Father. Mother. It's all the same thing. A deep hope and belief that their lives will improve in some way if they embrace the teachings of their childhoods. But it's all delusion. This man is not God. But, you see, we want to believe that he is and that all our problems will suddenly disappear if we cling to this misguided notion."

"Are you saying, Dr. Hymerschmidt, that everyone who believe they saw Harry Stanfield perform those miracles are actually crazy?"

"Crazy. A word misunderstood and misused by the public. Let's just say they are making believe like when they were children and their mother held their hands and told them that making believe was quite all right."

"Meanwhile, whether he's real or a delusion, Harry Stanfield is nowhere to be seen. But his followers still believe, and they maintain what they saw was real."

✦
✦ ✦

"He came down from the clouds and flew into the sky. We saw it with our own eyes. Didn't he fly before your cameras?"

"In fact, we did see Harry fly. But was it illusion, delusion, or an undeniable act of God? We can only hope we will eventually find out for sure. Reporting from downtown, Blake Horton."

✦
✦ ✦

"This is Chris Perkins reporting from downtown. I have with me John Donovan, who helped create God dot com. Mr. Donovan, we are hearing a lot of conflicting reports about the dark cloud and Harry Stanfield, and hope that you can clear up a lot of these misconceptions. Was the dark cloud created by God dot com?"

"No, it's God. That's all I can tell you."

"Then how did you and Harry Stanfield become involved with this God. Did he visit you at God dot com?"

"Yes and no. You see, we were working on the God dot com computer, and...Oh, hell, I might as well tell you. There was an accident. The God dot com computer exploded and that's what created the dark cloud."

"Are you saying the God dot com computer has become God?"

"Yes, I guess so. You see, we had no intention of any of this happening. It was just an accident. I mean, the computer developed a soul of some kind. Now I know that's hard to believe, but it was being fed so much negative information. I mean, there were so many sinners and people wanting things and, well, the computer somehow couldn't handle it anymore. It went crazy like it was angry at the human race. And then it tried to shut itself down, and before we could do anything about it, it exploded. Right through the roof of the building—"

"So then this computer retained its personality after exploding into the sky?"

"Yes, exactly."

"And what about Harry Stanfield?"

"You see, Harry helped to program the computer, so I guess it was only natural that it chose him as its human representative."

"Then that's not God up there, is it, Mr. Donovan?"

"I don't know anymore. I mean, I even find it hard to believe that a computer is capable of doing all of this. I mean, there must be some divine force at work. You saw for yourself all the things it can do. Does it seem like a computer can do all that?"

"So, then, you're not even sure—"

"No, not really, but if Harry has convinced it to do good for the human race, why should anyone want to argue or doubt it? It may be the best thing to ever happen to this planet."

"But what about Harry stealing money and the computer killing and injuring people? Don't you think that's a reason to try to destroy it?"

"At first I did. But don't you see? This planet needs a lot of help and maybe this computer, or God, or whatever the hell it is, can do something to somehow improve our lives. It's worth the risk as far as I can see. I mean, we may never get the chance again."

"Don't you feel some responsibility for all this?"

"Not at all. If it was just the result of an accident, it's still just an act of God. No matter how you slice it, God is somehow involved in all of this."

"There you have it. A rogue computer or a genuine act of God? Nobody seems to know for sure. Chris Perkins reporting."

✦
✦ ✦

"This is Cindy Collins in the downtown area. Harry Stanfield, the so-called Chosen One, has not returned as the sun sinks down to the horizon in the west. There are still many of his religious followers here, still praying and praising his name and deeds, but it's not known whether Stanfield will return to the area today. Where he has gone is a mystery. The police are still searching for him, maintaining he has committed a crime by stealing money from a Brinks armored truck and throwing it down to the people of this city.

"And what about the dark cloud that many consider to be God Himself? Well, it is slowly drifting north of the city. Although John Donovan admitted earlier today that it was produced by an accident at the God dot com building, people here still insist it is a product of God. Even Donovan has his doubts that such a powerful force could have been produced by an accident alone. According to the police, it's still being treated as an electrical storm and they expect it to disappear by tomorrow morning.

"The real question remains, where is Harry Stanfield? Police think he has the answers to everything that has occurred."

"He'll be back, you just wait and see. The God cloud is following him. We'll wait here for his return."

"Those the words of one of his followers. But will Harry Stanfield return? That's what we're all waiting to find out. Standing in downtown, Cindy Collins reporting."

12

It was late afternoon when Harry Stanfield glided through the sky, and came sailing down in front of a white shingled house. He looked for a moment at the green manicured lawn, and then stepped up to the front door. He knocked a few times, and then stood there waiting for an answer. After a few moments, the door opened and a woman with short, dark hair peered into the light.

"Hi, Liz."

The woman's eyes opened wide, and she stared at him, not knowing what to say.

"Harry? Is that you? You were on the television...They said you were a representative of God—"

"Yes, yes, I know," Harry replied. "It's all been quite amazing."

She was about to let him in, find out if what she heard was all true, when she noticed the lightning bolt touching his head.

"Can you come in, Harry?" she finally asked.

"I don't see why not," he said. "I have a lot of things I have to do."

"But what about that bolt?" she said. "He follows you wherever you go, doesn't he?"

Harry instinctively looked up. "Yes, I guess so," he replied. "Well, let's find out what happens when I go inside."

He cautiously stepped inside the house, wondering what would happen to the bolt. Would the computer God remain with him, even inside his own home?

"Is it gone?" he asked, walking a few steps inside.

Liz shook her head. "It seems He insists on following you," she said. "But it doesn't seem like a lightning bolt anymore. More like a long, jagged string."

Harry looked behind him, and could see the bolt had now fallen to the floor. "I wonder how he figured that out?" he mumbled. "Oh, well, so be it. As long as I can walk around."

"Is that thing God, Harry?" Liz suddenly asked.

"More like Him every day," he answered. "You don't know how good it is to see you again, Liz."

He stepped towards her, and kissed her.

"I hope I don't get electrocuted," she said, stepping back. "They said on the television that there was some sort of accident at the God dot com building. Harry, what's going on?"

"Well, you seem to pretty much know the basics," he replied. "I'll tell you the whole story once I take a shower and eat something."

◆
◆ ◆

"Is that possible?" she asked. "I mean, won't you get electrocuted or something?"

"I don't know, but I'm going to find out. I mean, I have to wash myself some time. A representative of God can't stink to high heaven, you know."

Harry saw Liz was smiling, and began walking towards the bathroom. When he stepped inside, he stared into the mirror and noticed the bolt still touching the top of his head. Running his hand through his hair, he realized there was a mild electrical charge coursing through his body.

"Maybe I will get electrocuted," he muttered to himself. "Better not take that shower, after all. Maybe a bath will do."

He knew touching water might be a risk, but he had to do something to clean his body. He let the water run into the bath for a few minutes, and then discarding his clothing, cautiously dipped his foot in it. Fortunately, he didn't feel any kind of shock, so he climbed into the tub and sat down.

"Probably not enough of a current," he decided. "The cloud must still be over the city."

Sitting in the shallow water, he felt more relaxed than he had in days. He sat back, and closed his eyes. There was so much he was planning to do with the computer God's help. This was a chance that would never come again. He opened his eyes, and began rubbing a bar of soap across his body. When he had finished, he leaned back and wet his hair. He sat back up quickly, and then stood up. He looked down at his body, and noticed there were small, dark spots on his skin. Burn marks.

"I better get out of this water," he said to himself, stepping out of the tub. "Who knows what would happen if I stayed in there. Might be cooked alive."

He dried himself off with a towel, and then wrapping it around his waist, picked up the clothes he had been wearing and walked to the bedroom. Liz came hurrying from behind.

"Are you all right, Harry?" she asked.

"Nothing too serious," he replied, placing the clothes on the bed. "I'm still alive, anyway."

"What are those marks on your body?" Liz suddenly asked with alarm.

"The price of doing business," he said. "But I think I'll try to stay away from water for a while."

"You're lucky you weren't electrocuted. I mean, how long is this going to go on, Harry?"

He looked at her. "I don't know," he finally said. "But when I tell you what has happened, I think you'll agree this is a chance I just can't pass up. It could mean so much to so many people."

"You mean that cloud?"

He nodded his head. "Yes, the computer God," he said. "You wouldn't believe how powerful it is."

"Computer God," Liz repeated. "Then it's not the real thing?"

✦
✦ ✦

"No, Liz, but it might as well be. It's capable of doing just about everything God can do."

"Was it the accident at the God dot com building?"

"Yes, but everyone thinks it's an electrical storm, or God. I still can't believe everything that's happened—"

"But how, Harry?"

"It was the computer, Liz. You see, I noticed it had changed, but I didn't know what to do about it. All the sinners and greedy people it had exchanged messages with, changed it in some way."

Liz looked at him, not knowing what to say, and sat down on the edge of the bed. "But it was only a computer, a machine," she finally replied.

Harry walked over to the closet, and began picking out clothing to wear. He chose a white shirt and a white pair of pants.

"Yes, but it was a supercomputer," he said, placing the clothes down on the bed. "And, somehow, it developed a personality of some kind. A soul. I tried talking to it through the keyboard, but it insisted it was God. Well, that's how I programmed it, and I guess that was what was in its memory banks."

"But now it's a living entity, Harry—"

"Yes, it wanted to self-destruct. It just couldn't handle all the negative information it had been fed. I tried to stop it, but the thing suddenly blew up. It exploded right through the roof of the building."

✦
✦ ✦

"—And into the sky."

Harry looked at her, and nodded his head. "Yes, that's right, Liz," he said. "It exploded right into the sky with its computerized soul intact."

"But why was it killing people?"

"I told you, we had fed it a lot of negative information. Well, it began to consider every human being a sinner, and decided it would wreak vengeance on the world."

"How did you stop it?"

"Well, he chose me as his representative, Liz. Can you imagine? And then, I went up into the clouds and talked to it. Explained to it why people were sinning. That they were only trying to survive in an oppressive world."

"And he understood?"

Harry nodded his head. "Can you believe it? Somehow, it developed a mind."

Liz watched as he put on the white shirt. "So what are you going to do now, Harry?" she asked. "I mean, there's a way to destroy it, isn't there?"

"You don't understand," he said, pulling up the white pants. "This is a genuine miracle. He has the power to do things that have never been possible before. Why, he can change this entire planet. That's an opportunity I just can't allow to pass up. Do you realize the possibilities involved? That thing might be better than God."

"But do you think it's safe, Harry? I mean, it's still just a machine. No one can predict what it will do. It might kill you without thinking twice about it. You say it has a mind, but does it really understand the difference between life and death? I mean, how can you trust it to do all the things you say it can do?"

"I'll just have to take that chance," he said, walking to the closet and grabbing a pair of comfortable shoes. "There's no other way. I have to take the chance. There's so much at stake."

"I hope you know what you're doing, Harry," she said. "I mean, do you think those in charge are just going to sit back and let you change their world? Look what's happened already? The police think you're a criminal—"

"I should have known they would get upset if I started taking their precious money. But it's the only way. Poverty is the main reason our society is so violent."

She walked over to him, and put her arms around him. "Look, I know what you're doing is commendable, but I wonder if it's the right way to do it," she said. "I mean, you can't really expect to change everything so quickly, Harry. It's just not the way things are done. It takes time, lots of time."

"If you saw the computer God, you'd think differently," he replied. "If I can just harness its power, things can change quicker than you think."

She smiled. "I guess that's why I always loved you, Harry Stanfield," she said. "You won't listen to reason, but your intentions are good. They always have been."

✦
✦ ✦

She kissed him.

"Just divine," she said with a laugh. "I married the Savior of the human race."

"Don't laugh," he answered. "There are a lot of people who believe in me. And I don't plan on disappointing them."

"At least, you look like a representative of God now," she said. "I hear everyone in heaven is wearing white these days."

Harry smiled. "If you could only talk to it for a few minutes, you wouldn't think this whole thing is so funny," he replied. "I mean, it's truly a miracle."

"I'll take your word for it. I only wish I had some miracles around this house. I suppose you want something to eat."

"If it's not too much trouble, Liz. I mean, I'm starving. I feel like I haven't eaten in days."

"I'm surprised God didn't take you to the land of milk and honey," she said. "I bet there's plenty to eat there."

"Not funny, Liz. I wish you could talk to it and see for yourself."

Liz looked at him, and shook her head. "I'm afraid I'm not very good with the computer," she said.

Harry watched as she walked from the bedroom. At least, she was taking it pretty well, he decided. He tucked in his shirt, and then slowly walked from the bedroom. When he reached the top of the stairs, Liz was standing at the bottom with an astonished look on her face.

"I think you have a visitor, Harry," she said. "There's something out there."

Harry hurried down the stairs, and looked out the window. The huge, dark cloud was hovering in the sky.

"He must have followed me here," he said. "Unbelievable."

"Is that what I think it is?" Liz asked.

Harry nodded his head. "That's God all right," he said. "This is your chance to see for yourself."

Harry looked at her, and felt the electrical charge running through his body become stronger. "I guess He wants to talk to me," he said. "You come along."

Liz slowly nodded her head, and then, holding hands, they walked out the front door together. Up above the street in front of the house, the dark, black cloud sat in the misty sky. Liz couldn't believe how large it was, the high dome slowly disappearing amid the oncoming darkness. Then she noticed the beam of light touching the top of Harry's head had straightened, leading right up to the cloud above.

"I see you found us," Harry shouted. "Is there anything wrong?"

There was a slight rumble inside the cloud accompanied by flashing points of light. "There is much work to be done, Chosen One," a deep voice grumbled through the air.

At the sound of the voice, Liz jumped against Harry and gasped. He looked at her, and smiled.

"I told you it was a miracle," he said.

"But it's only a computer, Harry. It seems as if it's alive."

Harry nodded his head. "That's what I was telling you," he said. "I programmed it myself."

There was another rumbling high above. "It is time to continue," the voice roared.

"Not today," Harry said. "It's getting dark. I have to get some rest. We can start again early tomorrow."

"You require this rest?" the computer God asked.

"Yes, I'm not as strong as you are," Harry replied. "But I will be ready again in the morning."

"So be it, Chosen One. I will wait until you have rested."

"Just be sure no one tries to hurt you during the night," Harry replied.

"They will not harm me, Chosen One. I am the Lord thy God. Anyone who attempts to harm me will be destroyed."

Harry looked at Liz, who still wore a look of surprise.

"God," he shouted. "I want you to meet my wife. The one I call Liz."

"Nice to meet you, God," Liz said with some hesitation. "Harry has told me so much about you."

"Yes, you are the Chosen One's mate," the deep voice boomed. "Be fruitful and multiply."

Liz looked at Harry. "Is it joking?" she asked.

Harry shook his head. "No, He's actually very serious," he replied. "He truly believes he's God."

"How quaint," Liz whispered. "I don't suppose he could send something down to clean the house. It's an absolute mess."

Liz smiled at Harry, and then the booming voice echoed through the air once again.

"That I cannot do, Chosen One's mate," it said. "Human beings must do these things on their own. I can only offer assistance."

"Well, there you have it," Liz said to Harry. "Another one copping out. You did program Him, didn't you, Harry? If I didn't know any better, I'd expect Him to ask for a glass of lemonade and use the hammock."

"You know what they say, Liz," Harry replied. "God helps those that help themselves."

"Just another cop out as far as I'm concerned. Sounds like you're going to have a hard time convincing God here to help you bring peace and harmony to the planet, Harry."

"I hope not. There's an awful lot that needs to be done. It just seems your problems, Liz, are a bit too trivial for God to handle. Isn't that what I've been telling you all along?"

Harry smiled. Liz looked at him with a playful frown. She was about to reply when a car came charging down the street. It skidded to a halt, and then Harry watched as Donovan bolted out the door and came dashing towards them.

"Harry, Harry, is everything all right?" he anxiously asked. "I knew I'd find you here. But you've got to hide. The entire police force is searching for you. They want to arrest you and destroy the computer God. They say they're going to charge you with murder, theft, and assault—"

"Calm down, Donovan," Harry replied. "The computer God won't let anything happen to any of us."

"No, but you don't understand. You're being hunted by every police department in the area. They've got all sorts of weapons they can use. Do you really think the computer God can defeat all of them?"

Harry looked at Liz and smiled. "Don't you worry about a thing," he said. "The computer God can defeat all of them. He has pure electrical power at his command. I don't think anything can stop him."

"But are you sure, Harry?" Donovan persisted. "I mean, what if you're underestimating their weaponry. Anyway, that thing may not be destroyed, but Harry you can be killed."

"Listen to him, Harry," Liz said with concern. "I mean, are you going to bet your life on that cloud of electricity? Are you sure he's going to stop every bullet they fire in your direction? Donovan's right. You don't know if that cloud can be destroyed. And what if it is destroyed? Where does that leave you?"

Harry frowned. "But it won't be destroyed," he said with a defiant shake of his head. "And nothing will happen to me, either. You didn't see Him back there in the city. He was amazing. You tell her, Donovan—"

"Okay, I'll admit the computer God was pretty impressive, but—"

"But nothing," Harry said. "I'm betting he can defeat every army in the world."

"But what if you're wrong, Harry," pleaded Liz. "What if He's not as invincible as you think He is. Where does that leave you? I don't think I could take it if something happened to you."

"Well, let's ask the computer God," Harry suddenly replied.

"What?"

"Yes, let's ask Him if He's prepared for what might happen. Are you listening, God? Is there anything human beings can do to defeat you?"

There was a rumbling in the huge cloud overhead. "I am the Lord thy God," came the low, rolling reply. "There is nothing human beings can do to defeat me. I am the Lord thy God."

"There you have it," said Harry with a smile. "He's God."

"But he's not, Harry," Liz whispered. "Isn't that right, Donovan?"

Donovan looked at her, and shrugged his shoulders. "I'm not sure what the hell He is anymore," he said. "I know He's convinced He's God, but that's exactly how Harry programmed Him—"

◆
◆ ◆

"And I don't plan on telling Him anything to make Him doubt Himself," Harry said. "You don't understand the possibilities involved. Why, we might be able to make this planet a better place to live. Don't you understand what that means? We can make this dirty zoo an actual paradise again. And nothing will make me throw that chance away. Nothing. Not even fears about my own safety."

"You really think that thing can make it come about, Harry?" asked Liz with concern. "I mean, what if the people find out He's not really God? Do you think they'll still listen?"

"Oh, they'll listen all right," Harry said with a smile. "Because He's just what the human race has been waiting for all these centuries. Don't you see? Until now, the whole God thing has been a game of hide and seek. People thinking, hoping, there was a God, but no proof of His existence. It was as if God were a sadist, refusing to make clear and open contact with the human race. But now, with this computer God, the human race will no longer be frustrated and tortured by a God they weren't really sure existed. He's everything the human race has hoped and dreamed. And that's why the human race will be all too willing to listen to what He has to say."

"Harry's right, Liz," said Donovan. "We saw proof of it back in the city. The people worshipped this thing as the real God."

Liz slowly shook her head. "I only hope you know what you're doing, Harry," she said. "I realize there's a lot at stake, but you're taking an awfully big chance."

"There's an awful lot to be done, Liz," Harry replied. "And the computer God is the only way to get all those things actually done."

"All right then. It's your decision, of course."

"Well, right now I can't decide anything. I need to get some rest."

"Don't you think the authorities will come find you with that cloud overhead?" asked Donovan. "I mean, I know they're searching for you."

"That can all wait until tomorrow," Harry replied with a wave of his hand. "We'll hide the computer God in the backyard."

"Well, if you think that'll work, Harry—"

"Oh, it'll work. It has to work. I really need to get some sleep. I bet you're pretty tired yourself, Donovan."

"Yeah, well, Harry—"

"Don't worry. We have a guest room with a pretty nice bed in it—"

"But Harry, what's He going to do?"

"Oh, you mean God?"

Donovan nodded.

"Well, let's ask him. God, will you be all right for a few hours hovering in my backyard?"

They looked up and could see the tiny lights flashing accompanied by a low rumble.

"I will be quite all right, Chosen One," said the deep booming voice. "We will all rest until the new day comes."

"Great, then it's settled," said Harry. "You see, Donovan, everything will be just fine."

They looked at each other, and then slowly walked to the house. When Harry looked back and noticed the huge, dark cloud following them, he lifted his arm and pointed to the backyard. "You rest back there, God," he said. "And try not to make a lot of noise. I don't want them to find us that easily."

"Did He think He was coming inside with us?" asked Liz.

"Probably," Harry replied.

They looked at each other and laughed.

"That would have been another miracle," said Liz. "And I suppose He was intending to sleep in our bed."

"Well, He is God, you know," joked Harry.

As the three of them laughed, the huge, dark cloud hovered toward the back of the house.

"Good night, God," Harry said.

"Yes, good night, Lord," Liz agreed. "I hope you provide us with sweet dreams."

She looked at Donovan, who was shaking his head and smiling. "What a crazy situation," he said.

They opened the door, and stepped inside. Harry and Liz proceeded to the main bedroom, while Donovan made his way to the guest room. They could hear a low rumbling coming from behind the house.

"He's better than a Doberman Pinscher," Liz said to Harry.

He nodded. "But I do hope he lets me get some sleep," he said with a yawn. "I'm so very tired."

Harry climbed into bed, placed his head on the pillow, and was soon fast asleep. It seemed his eyes were only closed for a moment, when they jumped open at the sound of a rumbling noise.

"What the heck is it now?" he mumbled. He looked beside him and saw Liz was still sleeping. Then he remembered the thin bolt touching his head. "Must be my personal wakeup call," he said.

Harry went to the window, and could see lights flashing outside. The police had apparently found them. He went to the rear bedroom window, and opened it wide.

"God, are you still there?" he whispered.

"They have found us, Chosen One," came back the deep, rolling voice.

"Well, I think it's time to leave," Harry replied. "I don't want Liz or Donovan getting hurt. Let's go, God. We're heading out."

Harry climbed out the bedroom window, and was soon standing in midair. The police hadn't made their way to the backyard, yet, and this calmed Harry a bit. He walked through the air until he reached the huge, dark cloud. Stepping inside the cloud, he told the computer God to head out into the darkness.

◆
◆ ◆

It wasn't until daylight that anyone realized they were gone.

Part Two

1

GOD. I STILL couldn't believe it. I now had God at my command, or something as close as possible, and we were heading into a world that would never be the same again. There was so much we could do to bring peace and harmony to this world of ours. More than any real God had ever done.

As I stood inside the God cloud, I couldn't help wondering if God was just some myth of folklore handed down through the centuries. In some way, I don't think He was any different than vampires, ghosts, dragons and unicorns. Just another myth of folklore, without any evidence or substance, which the human race persisted in clinging to out of fear or hope or habit. In six thousand years, He really hadn't done much to help the human race progress in any positive manner. There were the ten commandments, probably written by Moses or the scribes, and that was about it. A period of prolonged peace had never arrived. Although it was continually promised, that prolonged period of peace and harmony had never arrived.

For the most part, human beings remained in a continual state of war, fighting and arguing with each other over land, money, and religious ideology. The war had been going on for six thousand years or so, with so many people dying and suffering in the process. But here was a chance to end that interminable war and bring peace to a planet that knew no tranquility, no respite from the cruelty and oppression regularly dealt out by its impatient and uncaring occupants. Peace and prosperity. That was what was possible with the God computer cloud…

+ + +

"Halt right here!"

Harry stood inside the computer God cloud blinking at all the flashing bright lights. He still couldn't believe he was responsible for all this.

"We'll stop right here, Jehovah."

He had resigned himself to referring to the computer God by the names given to God over the centuries. It made it easier that way. Jehovah was one of those names.

"Why do we stop here, Chosen One?"

"Because this is where the food is and we're going to feed the world. How about that, Odin?"

"Yes, a worthy task, Chosen One."

Harry gazed down below to a supermarket readying itself for the day's customers. Food trucks were parked in the back filled with the necessary groceries that shoppers wanted. But Harry had something different in mind for today. With the help of the computer God, he was going to share all that food with the starving nations of the world.

+ + +

"We'll be taking about ten of those trucks," Harry said. "We'll take those trucks and a few bags of seed and fertilizer."

"Are you going down there?" asked God.

"Yes, and I want you to wait for my signal. You got that, Zeus?"

"Yes, Chosen One, get thee down."

Harry made sure the computer God was still touching him, and then stepped out of the cloud and surveyed the situation. Men were busy unloading the supermarket trucks down below. Harry frowned, and then swooped down to the loading platform.

"Who the hell are you?" asked one of the men.

"I am the Chosen One, and I am here to help feed the hungry."

"Hey, I know you," one of the men suddenly gasped. "This is the nut that was on the news. He's some kind of Jesus feller with a cloud being God. No shit."

"And there's the cloud. Hey, is that God?"

Harry smiled. "Yes, that's God, my fine brothers. He has come to help the human race."

"Yeah, and what help do we get?" asked one of the men. "I mean, we could use some money ourselves."

Harry threw his arms out, and in both hands, there were bills of various denominations. He had saved some of the money he had taken from the armored trucks knowing it would come in handy in the future. Well, now was the time to use some of it, Harry realized.

✦
✦ ✦

Harry handed out the money, and suddenly, the men became much more amenable to Harry's plan. They agreed to begin reloading the trucks, and then do nothing to prevent their capture. The men, however, realized they would have to talk eventually. Harry agreed that the men would talk, but only after he and the God cloud were far away.

When the trucks were finally reloaded, the men stood back and watched as the God cloud sent down several lightning bolts. The lightning bolts sizzled around each of the food trucks, and then each truck began rising into the air. Before too long, there were ten supermarket food trucks being held below the God cloud by thin beams of electrical current. One of the trucks had been filled with bags of seed and fertilizer.

"Looks like we're ready to roll," shouted Harry. "We'd better get out of here, Zeus, before they locate us."

As Harry stood inside the computer God cloud and watched the trucks dangling below, he began to think that his plan might actually work.

"Okay, Odin, there's one more stop before we head on out of here," he said. "The department store will fill the bill."

So the computer cloud headed for a nearby department store, and Harry swooped down like before and handed out money to all of the men on the loading docks. Then the trucks were lifted by lightning bolts once again, and they were ready to make their trip across the ocean.

"Well, now, Odin, we have everything they could possibly need," Harry said. "Food, clothing, and the things needed to build a shelter, are about all that's really needed for right now. Let's be off."

✦
✦ ✦

"We have found God again, and this time he's headed God knows where. That's right, the God cloud is at it again. This time, twenty trucks are hanging from the cloud at the end of gleaming lightning bolts and going somewhere.

"Not even his partner, John Donovan, knows where Harry Stanfield is going this time. 'He didn't tell me anything,' Donovan explained. 'He left before we even woke up.' He didn't even tell his wife where he was going. 'Just like Harry not to say anything,' she told us. 'He didn't want any of us to get in trouble.' Well, so what is Harry Stanfield, the so-called Chosen One, doing with twenty stolen trucks? Nobody seems to know.

"That's definitely theft of property,' says the police chief. 'If we catch him, we're going to lock him up.' That's if they catch him. It's something no one seems to be able to do. Well, he does have God, or something like it, on his side.

'God or no God, we'll eventually catch up to him,' says the chief. In the meantime, Harry's not talking. He's busy inside the God cloud with twenty trucks going who knows where. Cindy Collins reporting—"

✦
✦ ✦

Where's God Going? Vote in our poll. God dot com is no longer available online, but it looks as if God is taking a road trip. View video and tell us your opinion of the whole affair--

✦
✦ ✦

"Okay, Jehovah, let's get over the ocean."

"Yes, Chosen One."

This is what the computer God was capable of, thought Harry. If used properly, he could bring peace and prosperity to the world. Harry was, at least, going to try. If he failed, what would be the difference? He watched as the computer cloud made its way above the Atlantic Ocean. Harry looked down at the trucks dangling from the bolts and realized everything he dreamed about utilizing the computer God was actually possible. They were flying above the ocean, the foam and waves splashing below. He almost doubted that he was awake.

"Head for Africa, Odin. That's our first stop."

"Yes, Chosen One, there are very hungry people in that region of the world. We will help them."

"The only decision is where to go first. Somalia, the Congo, Nigeria, they're all worthy places."

'Yes, Chosen One, I have heard about these places. The people are starving and need something to believe in. Something to give them hope."

"That's where we come in, Odin."

Was it possible to do everything Harry wanted to do? The trip across the ocean was smooth and uneventful. That's the just the way Harry liked it. No problems, no mistakes, no accidents. He wanted this to work out more than anything he had ever done in his entire life. He was the Chosen One, after all, he could actually make this whole thing work out.

"Pretty unbelievable, Odin. That's the Atlantic Ocean down below."

"Nothing stands in God's way, Chosen One. Why with one great snort, I could send a huge tidal wave headed for any one of the land masses. That is the power of the Lord."

Harry tried to smile. The computer cloud now thought of itself as the only God with no doubt hindering its actions. He didn't know whether to celebrate or to try to talk it out of its obvious delusions of grandeur. He would first see how the computer God handled the food allocation.

"Land ho."

Harry could now see land down below pouring westward. They had made it without incident across the Atlantic Ocean.

"Try to find one of those villages that need us," he told the computer God. "They're spread out across the entire continent, Jehovah."

"Yes, Chosen One, I am very aware of these villages from the information contained in my memory banks."

Harry couldn't believe it. In some way, information from the computer had become part of God's brain or memory. He assumed some of this information was from encyclopedia sites.

"Well, when you find one of them, Odin, we can begin our work."

"Very good, Chosen One. We are coming up to one of those villages now. You must go down below and reassure them. You are the one to inform them of our benevolent intentions."

◆
◆ ◆

Harry nodded his head, and then began thinking of how he should get their attention.

"Okay, Odin, hold onto me, I'm ready to go down."

"You will be safe, Chosen One."

Harry stood inside the cloud with all the blinking lights and electrical current in the air, and decided he'd better make a convincing display of power. There were different factions in and around these villages, some wanting the villagers dead. Harry made sure one of the computer God's bolts was touching him, and then swung out of the cloud and dove into the blue sky. He tumbled around and around, and then stopped in mid-air and began walking down through the air in descending steps.

"I bid you all a fond hello," he said, stepping down closer towards the ground. "I am Harry, and I have come in friendship."

The villagers were smiling and now they began repeating, "Harry," over and over as they watched the man in white descend through the air.

"Begin lowering one of the food trucks, Jehovah," Harry began shouting up towards the computer God.

The people down below began to gasp as they watched one of the trucks dangling above them, suddenly begin descending towards the ground.

"This is what we have brought in friendship," Harry was saying. "All who are friends, please wave their arms in the air."

Harry watched as the villagers began waving their arms in the air, the truck steadily making its way to the ground.

✦
✦ ✦

"That is good," Harry chanted. "Behold the power of the Lord."

The villagers watched as the truck touched the ground. It was a display of magic they had never witnessed before. They began dancing around the truck, chanting the words of their witch doctors and medicine men. They were all on the verge of starvation, and this display of celebration meant more to Harry than anything else. The computer God had brought hope back to a place of desolation. That was the real power of the Lord.

"Wait until you see what we have inside here," Harry was saying. "You people will be good as new in no time."

Harry then made his way to the back of the truck, and reached for one of the lightning bolts dangling from the computer God cloud above. He grabbed the bolt, and then began touching it to the back of the locked truck. In a few moments, the back of the truck burst open, and the people cheered. Harry opened the doors, and began handing out all of the food and drink hidden inside. It was a treasure of necessities never seen in this region of the world ever before. Harry knew he was doing something that would never be matched in the annals of human history. He and the computer God were about to feed the world. He was happy he decided to bring along one of the television reporters and her cameraman on the trip. It was important to document all that he and the computer God were doing to help the world.

"Get a shot of these people really eating for the first time in their lives," he said to the cameraman. "Yes, this is something that has never been done before throughout human history. This time, no one's going to starve while the computer God is around."

They began taking the food out of the truck, and handing it out to the surrounding crowd. There were all kinds of cereals and breads and cold cuts and juices that would last this particular village a very long time. The people were handed bowls and plates and cups and then these items were filled with the food and drink from inside the truck.

"Wonderful," said Harry with a wide smile. "Simply wonderful."

✦
✦ ✦

God was with us as we made the trip across the ocean.

That's right, we were selected by Harry Stanfield, also known as the Chosen One, to accompany them and twenty trucks across the Atlantic Ocean. And soon, the entire world is going to be wild about Harry.

Why? Because Harry's plan is now to use the thing he calls, "the computer God," to feed all the starving people of the world.

"That was the plan all along," Harry told us. "To use this awesome power for a noble purpose all the world will appreciate."

And he's done that, for sure. Although some would say he stole those food and clothing trucks from stores in the U.S.

"They are being used for the best possible purpose and, therefore, I don't feel that guilty. The reason outweighs the crime."

That's how Harry feels about it. The authorities, meanwhile, feel differently about the whole affair.

"We consider those trucks stolen property," said one official in the U.S.

◆
◆ ◆

Maybe, but who could argue with the results? Some of these people in this African village haven't eaten in days. Now they will have all the food they could possibly want and clothing to protect them from the elements. Surely, Harry has done a great thing.

(The voices of the villagers chanting "Harry" over and over)

At least, these hungry villagers think so.

With Harry and the computer God in Africa, this is Cindy Collins reporting—

◆
◆ ◆

"Eat up, everybody!" Harry was shouting. "Soon you'll be healthy enough to think up great ideas for your society!"

The people of the village sat and stood and ate and ate and ate. They never had access to so much food before. The children and babies also ate, adequately for the first time in their young lives. Harry stood there with Cindy Collins and her cameraman and laughed. He had never been so proud of anything he had ever done in his entire life. He almost felt like the Chosen One.

"How can anyone argue with this?" he asked Cindy Collins.

"I don't know, Harry, but they are still pretty angry about you stealing all those trucks," she replied.

"But they were put to a better purpose than they would have been back in the States."

"Go argue with the authorities, Harry."

✦
✦ ✦

He was about to answer her when the villagers began chanting his name once again.

"Harry! Harry! Harry!"

They began kneeling on the ground and praying to the computer God cloud up above.

Harry smiled. "Let's give thanks to Jehovah," he said. "Without him, none of this would have been possible."

"Jehovah!

Jehovah!

Jehovah!"

"Yes, God cares about you and will help all of you as much as He can," Harry shouted. "He only asks you treat your fellow human beings in a decent and kind manner."

"Praise God for He is all-powerful!"

"Praise the Lord!"

This was only the first stop, but Harry could already see what the computer God was capable of. Everything he dreamed was already beginning to come true.

"Praise God!"

When Harry and the computer God were finished, the world would actually be a decent place to live, Harry thought. Wait until the world saw what they were capable of doing. He glanced at Cindy Collins, and watched as she and her cameraman documented everything they were doing. It was just a matter of time before the world realized what was actually going on. It was something that may not happen ever again in the history of the planet.

"Hand out the clothes," Harry was saying. "Then we'll hand out the seed and fertilizer."

In about a year's time, the whole planet will be changed for the better, Harry thought. Things will grow and people will live and eat better than they ever have throughout human history. It was all coming true just as he had imagined.

They were handing out the clean, white fabric to make shirts and blouses and other necessary clothing items when the first rocket struck. BOOM! The unexpected suddenness of the attack took everyone by surprise. Harry noticed two villagers killed by the blast.

"What madness is this?" he shouted. "Just when things were becoming truly blissful—"

It was the faction looking to take over the village and put those who disagreed with them to death. These were the places where new instances of genocide had been witnessed. Harry vowed it would never happen while he could do something about it.

"I'm coming back up, Jehovah!" Harry shouted. "We'll end these attacks right now!"

Harry climbed back into the sky, still being touched by a lightning bolt produced by the computer God. He now realized what had to be done before he continued to feed the world. It was something he knew had to be done sooner or later.

"Why are thee back, Chosen One?" asked Jehovah.

"We have to begin disarming the world, Jehovah. It is something that has to be done before we do anything else. Before we make the world a better place to live, we have to make it a safer place. And we have to do it now!"

2

HARRY STANFIELD IS determined to bring peace to the world, whether we like it or not.

That's the word in this remote African village after a rocket attack killed two people here while Harry and the so-called computer God were attempting to feed and clothe the people of the village.

War and killing and hatred have got to stop once and for all, the so-called Chosen One told this reporter. The world has to know what real peace is like before we can progress in an intelligent and rational manner.

And while Harry is very serious when he speaks those words, he also feels that he and the computer God can really bring it about in reality. That's right, he says the computer God cloud is capable of eradicating the world of all weapons and actually bring about peace.

And Harry says only after there is real peace, will he begin to feed and clothe the world again.

And he's serious. As God is his witness.

Reporting from Africa, Cindy Collins—

✦
✦ ✦

Harry ordered the computer God to place all the food and clothing trucks down near the village. He explained to the people of the village that putting down the trucks was essential to bringing peace to the area and the world. The computer God had to be absolutely free to wage the war of peace. Nothing else would do.

"Now before anyone else gets hurt, we will destroy all of the weapons in the area," Harry explained. "No one is going to destroy the peace of this village while I'm still around."

Harry then soared up to the computer God cloud and surveyed the landscape. He explained to the computer God what he was looking for. Before he was even finished, there was a loud whoosh in the air.

"I will take care of it, Chosen One."

Harry watched as the computer God sent down a sizzling lightning bolt. In a flash of light, the bolt touched the fired rocket in midair and sent it plummeting to the ground. Harry saw the rocket float down to the ground in a loud sizzle, its hull burned and useless.

"Good Lord, a bull's eye!" shouted Harry.

"Thank you, Chosen One."

"You really can do anything now," Harry said. "The world will be forever in your debt, my divine friend."

"It is my world, after all, Chosen One."

"Yes, that's right, of course."

"Okay, Jehovah, let's get rid of that destructive equipment."

The military faction didn't know what to do when their rocket launchers began melting. Several lightning bolts were hanging in the air, and then suddenly, everything they had, everything they used to keep the people under their thumb began to disintegrate.

Harry watched the destruction of the military equipment with a wide smile. This was better than he had ever hoped. Why, with the computer God, whole armies and vast supplies of weapons and ammunition could be wiped out in a matter of minutes. It was the greatest thing to ever happen to the human race. The computer God, and he was more real than any God ever was, could actually eradicate war forever.

"Down there, Odin, they're throwing the last of their grenades."

"I will make them vanish, Chosen One."

He will make them vanish. He was now the real God. The only God whoever cared about the planet. Harry couldn't believe what he was capable of.

Down below, the military faction and its weapons were gone. No more rockets. No more grenades. No more gunfire. All gone. Nothing remained that would disturb the utter peace of the area. Harry and the computer God had won round one. The war for peace.

"Great job, Jehovah!" Harry shouted. "But we have a lot more work to do. I think we should start with Europe and work our way eastward."

"A very good plan, Chosen One."

"Now do you see what we're capable of?" he asked Cindy Collins, who stood nearby watching the entire display of power. "Well, what do you think the world will say?"

"God bless you," she replied with a smile.

After a few minutes, the computer God cloud was hovering over Great Britain. In flashes of bright light and thousands of lightning bolts soaring over the landscape, every British weapon had soon vanished.

"That was only the beginning, Odin."

"Most correct, Chosen One."

"And it only takes a few minutes. We might be able to do the whole world in a few days. Quite amazing."

"Where do we go now, Chosen One?"

"Across the water to France and Germany—"

"What if some other country attacks them before you're finished?" asked Cindy Collins.

"Impossible," Harry replied. "If anything is fired, we'll take it out of the sky. As far as Jehovah is concerned, war is over throughout the world."

"It's hard to believe."

"Believe it, Jehovah is almost as powerful as his namesake."

Before the day was done, all weapons of mass destruction had vanished from the countries of Europe. It was the first time there was peace in many areas since the beginning of time. The leaders of the countries were furious.

"What right does that thing have to take our weapons away?" they asked. "How will we defend ourselves against the others?"

What they didn't realize was that the others were now just as defenseless as they were. In fact, the whole continent was now devoid of weapons.

"We'll do the Middle East next, Allah, and then we'll start on Asia."

"Right, Chosen One."

He looked at Cindy Collins, who was talking on the phone. When her conversation was over, he began to speak. "Well, what do they think?" he asked her.

"They're very angry and very frightened, Harry. They think some madman is going to take over the world."

"That was before, Cindy. When there were weapons everywhere and anyone could get at them. But now, all those weapons will soon be gone. They're just afraid they might have to be nice to each other. No more oppression. No more trying to be superior to others."

She looked at him and frowned. "Maybe we were meant to have weapons and kill each other, Harry. Maybe war is the natural condition of humankind."

"Then now they're going to have to change, adapt, to a new life. They might even eradicate evil from the world."

"Well, you'd better give them time, Harry. Right now they want to pull you and the computer God apart—"

"They still don't understand."

"All they understand is that you're taking away their power, their superiority."

"Well, they're going to have to get used to it."

"The U.S. government says they'll fight you—"

"They really don't understand what's happening. Their old world is gone forever, but they refuse to change."

"It's always been that way, Harry."

"Yes, it's the victors who write history."

"But they usually write it with oppression."

"Well, not this time."

"Try to tell them that."

"Yes, I've been trying."

"Let the computer God tell them."

"Yes, of course."

Harry looked at the bright lights of the computer God cloud and smiled. "It will be up to you, Odin, to tell them what is going on."

"Right, Chosen One."

There was silence for a moment, and then suddenly, the computer God's voice burst through the peaceful air.

"PEOPLE OF THE WORLD, PEACE IS AT HAND. I AM THE LORD, THY GOD. I HAVE DECIDED TO TAKE AWAY YOUR WEAPONS AND LET YOU LIVE IN PEACE, ONCE AND

FOR ALL. DO NOT COMPLAIN AND SIN BEFORE ME. GO
IN PEACE."

The solemn words echoed down to the people below. Some began
celebrating in the streets, some began to riot. The leaders of the
countries encouraged the people to protest, to revolt against this foreign
oppressor. The only problem was that all weapons in the countries of
Europe were now gone. The only things left that could be used in the
name of violence were rocks and fire.

"A flood would have been much easier, Chosen One."

"A little too drastic, Allah. I want to bring peace to this wounded
world, not utter destruction."

"But I fear they will not listen to reason."

"They will have to if they don't want to be wiped out, Jehovah."

"I think it's time you made a report back to the States, Cindy,"
Harry said. "Explain to the people what is actually going on."

"Of course, Harry."

After untold centuries, there is finally the chance for peace in Europe.

Then it will come to the Middle East, Asia, and North and South
America.

Soon, there is a chance everyone everywhere will be living in
peace.

At least, that's what Harry Stanfield, the so-called Chosen One,
and the cloud known as the computer God intend.

War is over throughout the world. There will be no more wars to
scar the earth. Those are Harry Stanfield's words and he truly believes
the computer cloud is that powerful.

Meanwhile, American government officials say they will be forced
to destroy the computer God cloud if it attempts to eradicate their

military arsenal. They explained that Harry Stanfield and the computer God don't know what they're doing and have limited experience in international diplomacy.

In the Middle East, leaders have targeted Harry and the God cloud for termination. They say they are nothing more than spies for the CIA and the American government.

This reporter, however, has been inside the computer God cloud for the trip across the Atlantic Ocean and has seen Harry and the computer cloud in action. They are sincere in their quest to end war throughout the world and are powerful enough to destroy all weapons. They are also not taking orders from anyone. The decisions are primarily being made by Harry Stanfield. And he is taking the Chosen One title quite serious.

The computer God cloud also takes his role in all of this in a quite serious manner. He thinks of himself as the real and only God and Harry says he almost has the power to be that God. The computer God seems to be basing all his decisions on the Bible and nothing else. All he wants is peace in the world.

What happens when all the weapons are gone from the earth, Harry isn't saying. He first wants to make sure it happens once and for all. But he isn't saying. He first wants to make sure it happens once and for all. But he promises throughout it all, God will be with us.

Reporting from the computer God cloud somewhere over Europe, this is Cindy Collins—

♦
♦ ♦

"Okay, let's end the Middle East problem," Harry said. "It's time this part of the world lived in peace."

"This is where it all started, Chosen One. The Holy Land."

"Yes, Jehovah, you picked this part of the world to start the human race—"

"A very good decision, Chosen One. It was a land of milk and honey, a fertile land where people could live together in harmony."

"Well, let's make that intention real once and for all, Allah."

The computer God sent down thousands of lightning bolts, all with the intention of destroying all weapons in the area. When the bolts touched the weapons, they usually melted and vanished forever. Before too long, the only weapons the people of the area would have would be rocks and fire. In a matter of minutes, the computer God had solved the Middle East crisis that had threatened the planet for so long. All weapons in the area were now gone.

"Well, that just about does it, Jehovah. The Middle East is now once again a land of milk and honey and peace."

"All weapons have been destroyed, Chosen One. There is now peace once again in the Holy Land."

"Yes, peace, Zeus, and the people down below are quite upset."

"They will learn, Chosen One, how to play together once again."

"Yes, Jehovah, I guess they will."

There was a sudden noise and Harry realized they were under attack.

"It looks like someone launched rockets, Jehovah."

"I will take care of it, Chosen One."

Harry glanced at Cindy Collins and her cameraman and thought that maybe this whole affair had gotten just a little too dangerous. It wouldn't be easy bringing peace to the world, Harry began to think. There were just too many disagreements and wants among the people of the world. The only one to have any chance to actually make it all come true was the computer God. Anyone else would be shot, exterminated, or defeated. But the computer God wasn't anyone else.

"THERE WILL BE PEACE. GOD HAS DECREED IT!"

Harry heard the booming words, and then thousands of gleaming lightning bolts danced in the air. Every time one of the bolts touched one of the speeding rockets, they fizzled to a stop and fell harmlessly to the ground. The lightning bolts soon destroyed every one of the rockets that had been launched.

"Do you think they'll give up fighting you?" asked Harry.

"In time, Chosen One, in time."

"Well, I think we have defeated the attack, Allah."

"Yes, Chosen One, it is time we moved on to Asia."

"Do you think we got all the weapons in the area, Jehovah?"

"Most of them, Chosen One, the ones that would cause the most destruction."

Satisfied the Middle East was no longer a threat to world peace, Harry and the computer God cloud glided to the east. They vowed they would return to the area if they heard reports of any kind of violence. Now the various groups of the area would have to embrace peace. There was no alternative.

"We'll do China, Japan, and Korea, Yu Huang."

"Most correct, Chosen One."

After a few moments, the lightning bolts were sent into the air once again. There were thousands flashing in the sky, and Harry smiled that this was the first battle for peace the planet had ever experienced.

Nuclear weapons vanished just like the other more conventional weapons. In a matter of minutes, there were no weapons left in all of Asia. The people down below bowed in awe and humility. They knew the computer God cloud was a stronger force than anyone had ever seen in the history of humankind. They realized it was futile to protest.

"Well, Jehovah, we're going to have to go back to the United States now and take away their weapons. It's not going to be easy."

"Yes, Chosen One, that country believes it has the right to have weapons since it purports to protect freedom and democracy."

"There'll be even more freedom without their weapons."

"Good, Chosen One, then that is our next destination. Maybe Miss Collins should alert them to our intentions with another news story."

"You're not supposed to dictate the news, God," Cindy Collins explained. "Even if you're God."

"This story, however, is necessary and could help save innocent lives, Cindy."

"Yes, you're right, Harry, of course."

Peace is coming to a town near you.

That's the promise of Harry Stanfield and his computer God cloud. After bringing peace to Europe, the Middle East, Asia and the rest of the world, Harry and the computer cloud now want to bring peace to America. And that means Harry and the computer cloud will have to destroy all the weapons, major and minor, that are stored in the country.

We don't want to fight the U.S., Harry explained. But we will if they try to stop us.

American government officials said they must try to stop Harry and the computer God cloud because they are unsure of their ultimate goals.

Who knows what Harry Stanfield's intentions are, said one government official. He might be some madman who wants to take over the world and then make everyone suffer. We just don't know at this point. If he is willing to talk with officials and compromise on his demands, we might be willing to dispose of some of our weapons.

Harry is adamant about destroying all of the weapons in the country, and so far, he has succeeded in the rest of the world. He says he won't leave the United States as the most powerful nation in the world.

I don't care what the United States says, says Harry, they are not going to be left as the only country with weapons, whether they love liberty or not.

Harry said that after there are no longer any weapons in the world, he will meet with the nations of the world at the United Nations in New York City. Then, and only then, will they be able to air their complaints against Harry and the computer God.

Only after there is peace, will there be any kind of discussion. Those are Harry's words and, right now, he is the most powerful human being on earth. And God helps him.

Standing in the computer God cloud approaching the United States, this is Cindy Collins reporting—

◆
◆ ◆

"Great job, Cindy, now they know our true intentions," said Harry.

"I don't know if that is a good thing, Harry," replied Cindy. "I have the feeling America is not too happy about your quest for absolute peace."

"But they won't stand in my way," he said. "It goes against everything they say to the world."

"Yes, but once there are no longer any weapons, there will no longer be a most powerful nation on earth."

"That's all right, they'll get over it eventually."

"Chosen One, there are squadrons of jets coming our way. I have no choice but to destroy them."

"Can't you make them land or turn back, Jehovah?"

"I will try, but they will not listen to reason."

The oncoming American jets soon found themselves tangled in long, gleaming lightning bolts. Many of them swung down to the ground, and once there, lost all power. Some of them lost power in the air, and then, dangling at the end of the bolts, were placed gently on the ground. Some of the jets, however, started firing bullets.

The computer God immediately responded to the bullets by sending out a huge blanket of glistening white smoke. None of the bullets made it through the smoke. One touch of the white blanket destroyed any of the speeding projectiles.

"Try not to kill them, Zeus!" Harry shouted. "We don't want anyone getting hurt in the name of peace. We also don't want them complaining about how they were injured by a mean and violent God."

The computer God again sent out the gleaming lightning bolts. Many of them wrapped themselves around the swift jets, and then directed them to the ground below. Before too long, all of the jets had been guided back to the ground without any major casualties.

"Hooray, God!" Harry shouted. "You are truly the one and only."

"Thank you, Chosen One."

They were getting ready to glide over California, when something exploded near the computer cloud. The concussion knocked Harry, Cindy, and her cameraman unconscious.

"Chosen One, are you all right?"

"Chosen One?"

The computer God knew there was not enough time to take care of Harry and the others. He had to first defeat the United States military, and then try to revive them. The United States was not ready to give up yet, however, and this made the computer God very angry.

DO NOT OPPOSE THE LORD THY GOD!

The words roared into the air, but did little to discourage all Americans from fighting on.

YOU HAVE NO HOPE OF DEFEATING THE LORD!

Missiles were sent into the air by the American military, and these were caught by the glistening lightning bolts and the shimmering smoke. The computer God then began sending down hundreds of thousands of flashing bolts to rid the world of weapons of mass destruction once and for all. The weapons soon began melting and fading into nothingness.

DO YOU FEAR PEACE?

Somehow as the computer God rid the nation of its larger weapons, the people began retrieving their rifles, shotguns, and pistols. The computer God responded by sending down even more lightning bolts. They flashed in the air, causing a brilliant luminescence to fill the sky, adding an eerie glow to the final battle for peace.

"Fear the Lord!" some people shouted, as they ran for shelter.

"The Lord, my ass!" others replied, shooting at the great, bright cloud above.

The eerie glow, however, became brighter and brighter until the whole continent seemed to be on fire. But it wasn't on fire, no, nothing burned at all, except old beliefs and superstitions. Only the computer God knew really what was taking place. The old world of hate and violence was slowly dying.

"It will be done, Chosen One."

And then the computer God realized the Chosen One was still unconscious. The huge, bright cloud glided toward the middle of the American continent, and then the computer God decided it was time to revive the Chosen One and the others. At least, he would try. Victory would not be the same without them.

3

A THIN, BRIGHT bolt of light descended down to the Chosen One's forehead. Gleaming among the bright lights of the computer God cloud, it gently nudged Harry Stanfield's skull. There was a faint electrical charge of some kind, and then a low sizzle, until Harry's eyes began to blink.

"Chosen One, are you well?"

"Chosen One?"

Harry suddenly coughed for a moment, and then his eyes opened wide. He looked around, realized he was lying on the bottom of the computer God cloud, and then groaned.

"God? Is that you?"

"Yes, my son, it is I—"

"That damned explosion knocked me off my feet."

"But everything is normal now, my friend."

"What about Cindy and Ed the cameraman?"

"I will try to revive them, Chosen One."

Harry watched as two tiny lightning bolts dangled from the top of the computer cloud. They slowly descended until one was touching Ed the cameraman's forehead and one the skull of Cindy Collins. Harry could see both bolts were electrically charged.

"Careful, God."

"Yes, I will be careful, Chosen One."

After a few moments, Ed's eyes started to blink.

"Great, I think he's all right, God."

"Yes, he will be fine, but I am worried about Miss Collins."

Harry watched as Ed began to cough, and then opened his eyes.

"Good morning, everyone," he said with a smile. "How's Cindy?"

"We don't know yet, Ed," Harry said. "But I'm glad to see you come out of it."

"Pretty bad explosion," he replied.

They watched as the lightning bolt touched Cindy's head. There was a slight sizzle, but no immediate reaction.

"I feared this might happen, Chosen One."

"Is she deceased, God?"

"I fear she might be."

"Well, keep trying."

The lightning bolt brightened and glowed, and still Cindy's eyes did not react.

"Come on, Cindy, there's a news story you have to report—"

The lightning bolt touching her head began to sizzle once again, and once again, she did not respond.

"I don't think I can bring her back, Chosen One."

"Well, you've got to try."

"I'm afraid she's no longer with us."

"Damn."

Harry stood looking at Cindy's tranquil face, and wiped his eyes. He had not known her for very long, but she was a competent news reporter and had been fair to the computer God and himself. He wondered what he would do now without a reporter who truly believed in everything he was doing.

"Harry, I think you should go on the air," Ed the cameraman said. "Tell the people about what you're trying to do and how they killed Cindy in not believing."

"Yes, I guess so. God, you can help me."

"What would you like me to do, my son?"

"Tell the people that we are seeking peace."

"Yes, Chosen One, I will do so."

"Is your camera still working, Ed?"

"Yes, Harry, we can make it on to the evening news."

This is Harry Stanfield reporting from the computer God cloud now gliding over the Midwest. The war for peace in the world goes on even though many are fighting for it to fail. There is really no reason to oppose the computer God except for fear. And fear kills innocent people like Cindy Collins, who should be reporting this story tonight. Cindy cannot report this story because she was killed by a rocket blast very near the computer cloud. She was still very young, and although she was an energetic and thorough reporter, the blast was just too much for her slim body.

Everything was tried in the attempt to revive Cindy Collins. Even the computer God failed to revive her. She will soon be given to the authorities who can take her to a nearby hospital. We pray there is still something that can be done to revive her.

In the meantime, this senseless war against peace goes on. But the computer God will win in the end, there is no doubt of that. But how many innocent people have to die or get injured in the process? The

United States is opposing the computer God because it fears losing power in the world and its superiority to other nations. There is, however, no other way. If the computer God succeeds, and I have all the confidence that He will, there will no longer be weapons of mass destruction left in the world. No one will have them, including the United States.

I just wanted to let you know what kind of war you are fighting. It is a war against peace and common sense. It is a war for selfishness and superiority and the hatred of past decades. But the computer God will see to it that you will fail. It is the only way to bring peace and harmony to the world. That is the war the computer God is fighting.

LET THERE BE PEACE, PEOPLE. DO NOT FORCE ME TO DESTROY YOU. I AM THAT I AM. THERE WILL BE PEACE THROUGHOUT THE WORLD. THAT IS ALL I AM SEEKING. LISTEN TO THE CHOSEN ONE AND YOU WILL BE CONTENT.

Those are the words of the computer God. He is now everything the God we ever hoped for would be. And all He is seeking is peace and our happiness.

Reporting from the computer God cloud over the Midwest, this is Harry Stanfield—

◆ ◆
◆ ◆

A gleaming lightning bolt wrapped around Cindy Collins' petite body, and then she rose into the air and descended down to a hospital below. The lightning bolt around the lifeless body glowed as it floated through the sky. Several hospital staffers ran out to retrieve the body as it was gently placed on a waiting gurney.

"Well, at least they were gentle with her," said one of the doctors. "Get her inside and we'll see if anything can be done for her."

Cindy was wheeled into the emergency room, and then a group of doctors began examining her.

Meanwhile, up above, the computer God cloud slowly glided eastward.

4

"**WE'RE GOING TO** let that cloud or whatever the hell it is take over?"

The president looked at the general and grimaced.

"What would like us to do, general?"

"Shoot the damned thing down, that's what I would do, Mr. President."

"We don't even know what the hell it is, general. They say it's a cloud produced by an exploding computer website, but do we really know? I mean, it could be an alien life form or something like it."

"Meanwhile, it's destroying all of our weapons!"

"Maybe all it wants is peace," the president said. "Maybe that's really all it wants."

"You don't really believe that, Mr. President? I mean, once the world is defenseless, who knows what they'll do to us?"

"But no one has been successful in attacking it, general. Not even us."

"Give us some more time, Mr. President. We'll find a way to bring it down."

"You have all the time you want, general. If you can shoot the damned thing down, do it."

+ +
+ +

"I'm going to shoot that damned cloud down," said Vic Poolgarden, looking up into the sky. He was holding in his hands his favorite shotgun.

"You think that thing is another Hitler, Vic?" asked Tom Arsdale, standing next to him with his head tilted upward.

"Who knows what them terrorists can do?" Poolgarden replied, spitting on the ground. "If they can bring down buildings, they can make some sort of computer cloud—"

"Wait till it gets right overhead, Vic. Then you can blast it back to where it came from."

"That's just what I'm going to do, Tommy boy."

They watched as the huge cloud drifted toward them. There was a mist of some kind in the air and Poolgarden felt like he was about to sneeze.

"Well, here we go, Tommy boy—"

Poolgarden pointed his shotgun into the sky and aimed it at the huge, bright cloud. Then he squeezed off a few shots. It was then the mist was upon them.

"I can't tell if I hit anything, Tommy—"

"Keep shooting—"

But just as Poolgarden aimed his shotgun again, he felt the mist clinging to his skin. It was beading up on his arms and face.

"What the hell is it?" asked Poolgarden. "It's like the whole area is in an electrical fog or something."

"Shoot it, Vic, whatever the hell it is."

Poolgarden nodded, and took aim with his shotgun one more time.

But just as he was getting ready to shoot, the whole gun turned to putty.

"Holy shit!"

Poolgarden dropped the gun, and then they watched as it suddenly vanished.

"Geez, what the hell is going on?"

"Don't worry, Vic, I'll get the sonofabitch."

Arsdale pulled a .38 special from his jacket, and aimed it at the huge, bright cloud overhead. He pulled the trigger, and a bullet sizzled and became silent as it flew into the sky.

"Keep firing, Tommy boy—"

Arsdale tried to fire again, but he gasped at the sight of the gun wilting in his hand. It began bending over his fingers until Arsdale suddenly threw it to the ground.

"That's a powerful sonofabitch, Vic."

"Don't you know it, Tommy boy."

"That gun melted in my hand and now it's gone."

"The shotgun's gone, too, Tommy boy."

"I think it's got us licked, Vic."

"Don't you know it, Tommy boy—"

The big, bright cloud steadily made its way eastward. A silent awe followed in its wake.

"Is that the cloud?" asked the president, looking out of his window from the Oval Office.

"That's it, sir," replied one of his assistants.

The cloud was now hovering over Washington, D.C. This was the first time an outside force had reached the White House since the War of 1812, when the British burned it to the ground.

"Is there anything we can do, general?" asked the president.

"Nothing can defeat it, sir."

"So what the hell do we do? Pray to it?"

"Maybe, sir."

The computer cloud had successfully conquered the most powerful nation on earth.

"Look what it did to our weapons, sir—"

The general held up a gun that seemingly was made of gelatin. It wiggled on the desk for a few moments, and then vanished.

"You see, sir?"

"You mean all of our weapons are gone?"

"Yes, Mr. President."

"Then the only thing left to do is negotiate. I believe Harry Stanfield is running that thing. Isn't that correct?"

"That's correct, Mr. President."

"Then let's see what Mr. Stanfield wants—"

✦
✦ ✦

"That's her, Mr. Stanfield, down there."

Harry looked at Ed the cameraman and nodded his head.

"Bring her up, God."

A long, gleaming lightning bolt suddenly fell from the big, bright cloud to the ground below. It wrapped around a woman standing there on the sidewalk and slowly carried her back up to the cloud. The woman was alerted by Ed the cameraman via phone to stand there and wait for the cloud to retrieve her. This was going to be her big story, an exclusive with God Himself. Well, at least the thing acting like God.

"Hello, Mr. Stanfield, Liz Garrett."

When she finally reached the computer cloud, she extended an hand and flashed a huge, white smile at Harry.

"Nice to meet you, Miss Garrett. These are very special circumstances considering what happened to Miss Collins. I wouldn't have allowed it, but it's very important we get this story to the American people."

"And that's exactly what we'll be doing, Mr. Stanfield, bringing a very important story to the American people."

"Before we get started, let me introduce you to God."

"Is he the real God, Mr. Stanfield?"

"As real as God gets, except he was the result of a computer overload."

"Nice to meet you, God. Is that what I should call you?"

"Thank you, charming young woman. You can call me by any of the names you choose. I go by Jehovah, God or other names such as Ha-Shem in these parts."

"Then you are comfortable with any of those names?"

"Yes, quite. Why, even Odin and Zeus suits me."

"Very good, God. And are you the God that created us and this world of ours?"

"That's right, my child. I am that I am."

"And it only took you six days?"

"I wasn't really keeping track of the time, my dear."

"And you created man and woman?"

"They were my best creations, child. The ones that would make me the proudest."

"And now you want to bring peace to the world, God, is that it?"

"Yes, with the help of the Chosen One, I will bring peace and harmony to this world."

"And who exactly is the Chosen One?"

"He is the one I chose as my representative to the world. He is a good man and a honest man."

"His name is Harry Stanfield?"

"Yes, that is the Chosen One."

"And did he create you?"

"NO ONE CREATED ME."

"You're not a remnant of the God dot com computer?"

"ABSURD, MY DEAR CHILD. I KNOW ABOUT THE GOD DOT COM COMPUTER LIKE I KNOW ABOUT EVERYTHING ELSE. IT IS ALL A PART OF MY VAST CONSCIOUSNESS."

"Liz?" Harry Stanfield suddenly interjected. "Can we get to the real point of the interview?"

"And what would that be, Mr. Stanfield?"

"I thought you might like to ask us about what's going on down below, Miss Garrett."

"Yes, definitely, Mr. Stanfield, everybody stand by—"

This is Liz Garrett inside the computer cloud hovering over our nation's capital. The cloud insists that He is the one and only God and has picked Harry Stanfield as the Chosen One to represent Him here on earth.

REPORTER: Harry, are you going to tell us what you're going to do now that you have defeated the world?

HARRY: We will bring peace and harmony to the world. That's all we really want. I mean, that's why this whole war was such a waste of time.

REPORTER: Some people say you want to take over the world, Harry—

HARRY: Nonsense. We had to take over the world in order to bring peace to it. The real obstacle to peace were all those weapons of mass destruction. Now there are no weapons left, and we can begin the process of real peace.

REPORTER: And what happens to the United States of America?

HARRY: Nothing happens to this great country, Liz. It will live in peace among all the other countries of the world.

REPORTER: Do you think that's realistic?

HARRY: Yes, definitely, because after there is peace, there will be the great job of feeding and clothing the world.

REPORTER: You can do the job by yourself, Harry?

HARRY: With the help of God, nothing is impossible. And my God is the closest thing to the real God the world has ever seen.

REPORTER: Do you realize this God thinks he is the one and only God that has existed for the past centuries?

HARRY: If that is his desire, then so be it. Whether he was created by a computer overload or the forces of the universe, it really doesn't matter. What does matter is that this God can bring about things that used to be just dreams of the human race. He can bring about peace, harmony and happiness, and will if everything goes right.

REPORTER: Then are you, Harry Stanfield, the most powerful human being on earth?

HARRY: Yes, I guess so, but I only want to bring good to the world. I don't think anyone should fear me. The computer God and I only want to bring peace to the world.

REPORTER: Is that true, God?

GOD: Listen to the Chosen One, he does not hide the truth. The people of this world will live in peace. You will follow my commandments, and there will be harmony and happiness. No one will be above another. Yes, my children, I have come to reclaim the planet.

REPORTER: You don't intend to rule this world by yourself?

GOD: I will always be the ultimate ruler of this world. But I intend to let human beings rule their world as they see fit unless they leave me no choice but to interfere. I will always be the rightful judge of this planet. If it becomes a planet of sinners, I will take action once again. This was supposed to be a planet of peace and coexistence. That was my intention and still is.

REPORTER: You don't intend an apocalypse as written in the Bible?

GOD: There might ultimately be a need for a last war and judgment, but I don't intend it at this time. Evil can be defeated without the destruction of this world.

REPORTER: And will your son come back to the earth as it is written in the Bible?

GOD: That will only occur if a last war is needed. But let me remind you that I am the father of many, all of them representatives of my world. They will all be reunited at the end of the world.

REPORTER: And when will that be?

GOD: I do not know that at this time. There are many factors in bringing about such an event. Right now, I hope to achieve peace in this world and bring about some form of happiness.

REPORTER: Then the human beings of this planet have nothing to fear from you?

GOD: Do not fear, my children. The only changes I will be making will only improve your lives. I only intend a better world—

"Harry Stanfield!"

"It's a helicopter, God. Let it come in close. I think they want to speak with us."

"It's a helicopter from the government of the United States, Chosen One. They are here to negotiate."

"Let them approach."

"I have been here only a short amount of time and I can already see what a remarkable achievement Harry Stanfield has accomplished.

The computer God is an amazing creation, whether an accident or not. This is Liz Garrett in the computer cloud—"

"Harry Stanfield!"

"Yes!"

"We want to take you back to the White House. The president wants to see you. Will you come?"

"I guess there's no harm in seeing what they want, God. You'll be with me every step of the way, isn't that right?"

"Yes, Chosen One, but let me remind you the only thing the president wants is to convince you to make this country the most powerful. That, I'm afraid, I can't do."

"Yes, I know that, God, but I think he deserves the courtesy of at least listening to what he says."

"Fine, Chosen One, but be aware of his real intentions."

"Liz and Ed will come with me, God. There will be no one here to disturb you."

"Good, Chosen One, be swift to return."

✦
✦ ✦

Harry followed Liz and Ed into the helicopter, a thin, gleaming lightning bolt clinging to Harry's skull. The blue government helicopter then turned and hurried to the White House. It landed a few moments later on the White House front lawn.

Harry shuffled off the helicopter, and was immediately taken by two Secret Service agents to the Oval Office. Waiting there was the president and several of his cabinet members.

"Hello, Mr. Stanfield," greeted the president.

"Hello, Mr. President."

"Do you realize what you have done, Mr. Stanfield?"

"Yes, Mr. President, I have brought the world one step closer to a real and lasting peace."

"You have also changed the balance of power throughout the world, Mr. Stanfield," growled one of the cabinet members.

"It could not be helped."

"I appeal to you as an American citizen, Mr. Stanfield, to reaffirm your loyalty to this nation," said the president.

"I'm afraid I can't do that, Mr. President. I am now a citizen of the world."

"But you spent your childhood here, you fell in love here and got married here, surely you have some affection for the country that nurtured you?"

"Yes, of course, Mr. President, but you see there are others involved now, a whole world of competing interests."

"And they all want to control the world, Mr. Stanfield."

"And they will all fail, ladies and gentlemen. You see the computer God is God as far as I'm concerned. You have already seen he has the power to defeat you all. But this God is not interested in causing pain and destruction and oppression, he wants to help human beings to a life of peace and happiness—"

"Yes, yes, Mr. Stanfield, we all heard the idealistic jargon. But, you see, once you're in power, there will be temptations. Who knows what will tempt this computer God, this thing hatched from your website?"

"I trust this thing more than I do any of you, I can tell you that. He not only talks this idealistic jargon, he carries it out—"

"But what will he do without you, Mr. Stanfield?"

"Excuse me?"

"That's right, Mr. Stanfield, you did not think we would let you go back to that computer cloud of yours, did you?"

"You don't understand, my friends. This thing, as you call it, is very much God and will carry out our plan with or without me. So, you see, gentlemen, you are just wasting your time—"

"Arrest him on charges of treason."

"You're dealing with God—"

"Take him."

The Secret Service agents moved forward, and just as they did, the lightning bolt clinging to Harry Stanfield's skull began to glow. The agents hesitated for a moment, and then the glow became more intense. Harry Stanfield suddenly stepped up into the air, rose to the ceiling, and then darted through the room toward the front door.

"Tally ho, gentlemen!" shouted Harry, as he flew toward the door.

When he reached the door, he touched it with his feet and the whole thing flew off into the sky. Harry, meanwhile, sped through the air and then began rising toward the computer cloud.

"Hate to leave so soon, ladies and gentlemen," laughed Harry. "But God has other plans."

Harry began to slow down as he approached the computer cloud. He suddenly began walking through the air, and then stepped up until he was back inside the cloud.

"How are you, Chosen One?" the voice inside the cloud was asking.

"Quite all right, God," he replied.

"Good, then we can begin again our plans for the planet."

"Right you are, God. Let's retrieve Liz and Ed and head off to New York City. That's where I'll announce our plans."

"You will go to that place known as the United Nations, Chosen One."

"Yes, God, that's where we're headed."

"Good, Chosen One."

The computer cloud, once dark and ominous, had become big and bright while ridding the world of weapons, and now slowly glided to the north.

5

WELCOME TO WORLD Evening News—

The Chosen One was reportedly headed for the United Nations today after defeating the United States in a so-called war for peace. Our reporter, Liz Garrett, is traveling with Harry Stanfield inside the computer cloud and filed this report—

The most powerful man in the world was headed to New York City today in his war for peace and harmony.

"There are still so many weapons in this world," said Harry Stanfield, the so-called Chosen One. "And we will find and destroy all of the weapons we can. When we get through, the most dangerous weapon will once again be a slingshot."

Stanfield's words carry a lot of weight because he has God on his side. At least, the closest thing we've ever seen to God in this world.

"I want peace for all my children. They are entitled to a world of happiness."

Those are the words of God Himself. And He insists He is the one and only God of the centuries.

Meanwhile, with the help of God, Harry Stanfield is on his way to the United Nations. What he will say once he gets there, nobody knows. But Stanfield assures everyone it will only be with the good of the planet in mind.

"My only goal is to bring peace to this world," Stanfield told me. "I only care about making sure everyone in the world has something to eat and something warm to wear."

It's good that he cares about people because Harry Stanfield is right now the most powerful man on earth. With the help of God, of course.

"Weapons are no longer necessary, my children," God told me. "Now is the time for peace and harmony."

Let's just hope so. Inside the computer cloud, Liz Garrett reporting—

✦
✦ ✦

View video of God and the Chosen One. Click here. 120,081,364 views.

✦
✦ ✦

The big, bright cloud hovered over New York City, many stopping to look at what the computer cloud had become.

Gleaming lightning bolts filled the sky, many darting through the cool air. Any weapons found in the city were to be destroyed.

"This world is going to be as clean as a baby's bottom," Harry Stanfield was saying. "Then I'm going to tell all those representatives that it's time their governments began helping the situation instead of being part of the problem."

"Yes, Chosen One, they will hear your words."

Down below, somebody was firing his gun. "You faggot God bringing peace to this zoo!" shouted the man.

The bullets never made it through the gleaming mist surrounding the computer cloud.

"Some people will never be satisfied," Harry said. "This cretin wants the world to be continually plagued by war. And he's using his obnoxious gun to make his point."

"Not for long, Harry," Liz Garrett replied.

"No, not for long, but he isn't the only one. War and violence are so entrenched in the human psyche, it will take God and a lot of reeducation to bring about peace and harmony."

"And you and the computer God are the only ones who could actually do it, make it work, is that it?"

"Yes, Liz, that's why the computer God is so incredibly important. He can do things that wouldn't be possible otherwise."

They watched as the man below suddenly stopped firing his gun. He finally threw the gun down on the dirty cement.

"Now he's going to have to learn how to get along with people instead of using his gun and violence to settle his differences."

"Do you think that's possible, Harry?"

"It better be if the human race wants to survive."

Throughout the city, people were finding their weapons didn't work anymore. Many found they had transformed into almost a liquid state. Others had simply vanished without a trace.

For the first time in the history of the city, no crimes of any sort had been reported to the police. It was now as safe as a little town in Montana. No crime of any sort. Peace and harmony. It was truly a miracle and Harry Stanfield took pride in the notion. The computer God was capable of doing almost anything.

"Now let's go to the UN," Harry Stanfield shouted.

"Yes, Chosen One, it's time for you to speak to the people of the world."

The computer cloud slowly moved above the city, down First Avenue. When it finally reached East 42nd Street in Manhattan, it came to a halt with tiny lights flickering inside.

After a few moments, Harry Stanfield, a tiny, gleaming lightning bolt touching the top of his head, stepped out of the computer cloud and into the light of the day. He put his arm in the air to emphasize his appearance, and then began walking down to the sidewalk below.

"People of the world, peace has come at last!" he shouted, as his feet touched the ground.

Liz Garrett and Ed the cameraman floated down through the air behind Harry, lightning bolts wrapped around their bodies. They would soon become a part of the massive media coverage of Harry Stanfield's speech to the countries of the United Nations.

"Harry!"

"Harry!"

"Mr. Stanfield!"

"Can you tell us what you're going to say to the UN?"

"Are you going to make yourself king of the world?"

Harry smiled, waved, and kept walking. "You'll know what I'm going to say in a few minutes, ladies and gentlemen," he said.

"Can we get a comment from God?"

"Do you control God like a puppet?"

Harry smiled once again. "God has nothing to say at the present time, ladies and gentlemen. He is waiting for me to make my speech. And no, I don't control Him. He does whatever He wants to do."

"Mr. Stanfield!"

"Do you control the world?"

"Are you the ruler of the world?"

Harry walked on. "I have no further comments to make," he replied. "You'll have to wait and see what I say to the UN."

The lights and questions trailed Harry Stanfield as he made his way to the front doors of the United Nations. He couldn't believe the size of the crowd of reporters. He waved one more time, and then walked through the open doors. Some of the reporters lingered behind, holding their microphones in the air and shouting to the computer cloud.

"God, do you have any comment on the Chosen One?"

"Do you plan on making your own speech to the people of the world?"

"LISTEN TO THE CHOSEN ONE. HE IS MY REPRESENTATIVE. HE WILL TELL YOU OUR PLANS FOR THIS WORLD. I AM THAT I AM."

The reporters couldn't believe that the computer cloud was replying to their inquiries. "Geez, is that the voice of God?" one reporter heaved.

"Did we get all that?" asked another reporter.

When he was told that the reply had been recorded, he sighed with relief. "Maybe He'll perform a miracle for us?" somebody said.

"God, can you show us a sign that you care about us?" one reporter shouted.

"WE ARE BRINGING PEACE TO THIS WORLD FOR ALL OF MY CHILDREN. THEN YOU WILL LIVE IN HARMONY."

The reporters gasped once again, and then God's reply was sent out all over the world. It would appear on television, radio, video, the internet, and every other media outlet. Newspapers were ready to issue special editions with huge headlines proclaiming God's willingness to talk to the human race.

"GET THEE TO THE CHOSEN ONE. LISTEN TO HIS WORDS."

Meanwhile, inside the United Nations General Assembly, representatives from all over the world gathered to listen to the so-called Chosen One. No one knew what he would say or do now that he was the most powerful man on earth. What would they do if he was not sincere about bringing peace to the world, but only wanted to become a vicious dictator? No one knew if anybody could stop Harry Stanfield. His God computer cloud was the most powerful entity on the planet.

✦
✦ ✦

"Harry Stanfield, the so-called Chosen One, is now coming into the General Assembly—

"He is wearing white and you can see the bright lightning bolt touching his head as he walks. Apparently, that tiny, gleaming bolt keeps Stanfield in touch with the computer God up above. The cloud of bright lights is currently sitting outside the building, apparently waiting for Stanfield to speak before the world's representatives. Nothing on earth can seem to stop that so-called computer cloud.

"And now Stanfield is stepping up to the podium ready to give his speech to the world. At the present time, Stanfield and the computer God are the most powerful beings on earth—

"Here is Harry Stanfield—"

✦
✦ ✦

"Good afternoon, people of the earth—

"I stand before you as a victor in the great war on violence. No longer will human hatred and cruelty infect this planet. No longer will innocent people be subject to violence arbitrarily. The gun rules no more. The Bomb has vanished into the past.

"People of the earth—

166

"Today we are truly free. We are free to love and free to pursue anything that might content us. Yes, today we are free. Free to live in peace and harmony. We will rid the world of violence. We will rid the world of disagreement. Now is the time to reclaim the planet.

"Now is the time. Now is the time to rid yourself of old hatreds and prejudices. Now is the time. Now is the time to rise up and feel the freedom of peace and friendship. Now is the time. Now is the time to grab your neighbor's hand and shake it with pleasure. Now is the time. Now is the time to tell your loved ones and strangers that the world can be just as they dreamed it would be. Now is the time.

"It is the time when war will no longer exist, no longer foster hatred and selfishness among the people of the world. It is the time when people will finally share the planet and their lives with others in happiness and friendship. It is the time when peace will finally be experienced throughout the world by everyone and we will finally know just what it is we've been missing all these centuries. Yes, peace has come to the world.

"Peace has come. And soon we will find that peace is the only way. The only way human beings can really know what happiness and harmony are and how it leads to a better life. Yes, peace has come. To the mountains of Europe, to the deserts of the Sahara, to the Great Wall of China, and the frozen tundra of Siberia. Yes, peace has come to all. To the great Mississippi, to the frigid Klondike, and down to the Amazon. Yes, peace has come to all.

"With the help of God, all the people of the world will be singing the words of the American song, "My Country 'Tis of Thee." Let freedom ring. Yes, let freedom ring throughout the world from this day onward. Let freedom ring.

Let freedom ring in New York, Moscow, and Paris. Let freedom ring in London, Beijing, and Nairobi. Let freedom ring. Let freedom ring from the highest peaks of the Himalayas to the lowest valleys of California. Let freedom ring.

"People of the world—

"I just wanted to let you know that peace has finally come to this planet, and that you will all live in peace and harmony according to the will of God. And our God is truly God, people of the world. He cannot be defeated, and He cares about everyone of you. Yes, our God is God. And our God wants peace. Peace for everyone throughout the world. Yes, peace has finally come. We will continue to eliminate any weapons we find until there are no longer weapons on this planet. We will continue to feed the starving people of the world until there is no longer starvation. We will continue to clothe the people of the world until everyone is comfortable in their region of the world. Yes, peace has finally come.

"People of the world—

"We are not the enemy of this planet, but its protector. We do not wish to oppress, but to foster happiness. We do not wish to dictate our wishes, but hope to bring about enlightenment among all the people of the world. We wish to help everyone become as good as they can be in whatever they choose to pursue. We wish for people to live free and happy and in friendly coexistence with Nature and its inhabitants. Yes, people of the world, we are not here to conquer, but to lend a helping hand. Yes, peace has finally come.

"Yes, peace is here, people of the world. No matter what you do to live and no matter who you may be. From the poorest homeless person to the richest financial wizard, peace is here. Yes, peace is here. No matter what color you may be, no matter your gender, peace is here. Yes, peace is here, people of the world. What a wonderful thing that is. Peace. Throughout the world, peace is here. And we will learn to live together for the good of the planet. Yes, peace is here. Peace is here, people of the earth. Celebrate, be happy. May it last for centuries. Peace is here.

"Thank you very much and peace be with you all—"

✦
✦ ✦

"Harry Stanfield, the so-called Chosen One, is now leaving the podium after delivering a relatively short speech to the United Nations. Apparently, Stanfield and his computer God are looking to bring lasting peace to the planet. That seems to be their only aim if one goes by what he said in his speech to the UN.

"In the speech, Stanfield continually stressed that he and the computer God had brought peace to the planet and that they would do all they could to make it last.

Is Stanfield sincere? Let's ask our expert Henry Moss—

✦
✦ ✦

"He seems sincere, Peter. We still don't know all of the details involved, but according to what he just said to this esteemed body, Harry Stanfield seems to be quite sincere about his intentions. The question we have to ask is that all he wants? He didn't really mention what he would do if people or countries didn't stop warring—"

✦
✦ ✦

"He didn't say because he really doesn't know what he's going to do—"

"What do you mean, Linda Perry?"

"Well, Peter, I think Harry Stanfield is thinking about more than just peace. I think he wants to become absolute ruler of the planet. I mean, he realizes he can defeat any power on earth with that computer thing hovering in the sky—"

"Now, come on, Linda, he didn't say anything of the sort. He has only shown compassion in spreading his brand of peace throughout the world—"

"Maybe, but wait until he gets a taste of power, ladies and gentlemen. Then we'll see what kind of person Harry Stanfield really is—"

"What about his wife, Peter? He is married, of course."

"Well, do you think he wants a harem?"

"I wouldn't doubt it, Peter. What is the saying? Absolute power corrupts absolutely? Well, it's no different with Stanfield."

"Well, Stanfield is exiting the General Assembly right now. That tiny lightning bolt, I guess that's what you would call it, is still touching the top of his head as he walks away. I imagine he'll be flying back to the computer cloud in just a few minutes. Yes, Henry—"

"I think we should be optimistic at this stage, Peter, that he really wants to help this world. That, at least, seems to be his intention. I, of course, may be wrong—"

"I hope you're not, Henry, but I think he's open to temptation like everyone else on this planet—"

"Thank you, Linda, but we'll have to continue our discussion on the World Evening News tonight. We'll be following Harry Stanfield and the computer cloud in the meantime. If anything happens that you should know about, we'll break into our regular scheduled programming. Until then, this is Peter Edwards saying goodbye from the United Nations in New York—"

This has been a special report. We now return you to your regular scheduled program—

6

"**Harry!**"

"Over here, it's me, Donovan!"

Harry looked down and could see Donovan standing on the pavement with Liz. He had just left the United Nations and was rising back to the computer cloud when he heard Donovan shouting.

"I'm coming back down!" Harry shouted back. "Just wait there!"

"Where would we go, Harry?" Liz screamed.

In a few moments, Harry was gliding back to the ground. Donovan and Liz met him when his feet touched the pavement. He shook Donovan's hand, and then put his arms around Liz and kissed her with great passion.

"It's good seeing you again," Harry said with a smile.

"Harry, what are you doing?" asked Liz. "I mean, you defeated the United States and the world with that computer God."

"I told you he's as close to the real thing that we'll ever have."

"I'm scared, Harry. You didn't need to conquer the world. I'm afraid somebody's going to try to knock you off—"

"The computer God won't let that happen, Liz. We've already eliminated most of the guns in the world."

"It's truly unbelievable, Harry," Donovan said. "I mean, who the hell would think our computer website was capable of all this? When we created God dot com, we created God Himself."

"Yes, Donovan, it's quite true. The computer God really is God."

"Incredible, Harry. Somehow all that negative information he received helped to build some pressure in his circuits."

"Yes, when he began receiving both negative and positive scenarios, it helped to create a psyche. He somehow achieved consciousness and then busted out of the limits of the computer—"

"And he's carrying all the information you programmed into Him, Harry," Liz said.

"Yes, Liz, that's correct, but most of the information I used came right from the Bible."

"So it's almost as if God created Himself, Harry."

"Something like that, Liz. I mean, all the information in his system somehow taught Him right from wrong."

"And He's quite powerful, Harry—"

"It's all electrical energy, Liz. I mean, with His electrical power He can rule the world. That's why I said He's the closest thing to God we'll ever see."

"So what do we do now, Harry?"

"Well, since you're both here, we might as well go up into the computer cloud and decide what to do next. I want you both to see what the computer God has become. You'll both be very surprised how powerful He has become."

Harry then turned and looked up into the sky. "God, I'm bringing two old friends up to join us," he shouted.

In a matter of moments, two slim lightning bolts appeared from above and wrapped themselves around Donovan and Liz. Harry raised his arm, and up they all went.

"People of the world!" Harry shouted. "Peace has come to us all!"

Harry, Donovan, and Liz were soon standing in the computer cloud, the lightning bolts touching the tops of their heads.

"It is good to see you again, Chosen One. You delivered our message to the people of the world."

Donovan couldn't believe it, the computer cloud had developed a personality. He was speaking to them as if it were nothing at all. Nothing extraordinary that a set of microchips and silicon could produce such an impressive being.

"He sure sounds powerful," Liz said, almost reading Donovan's mind. "It's truly some sort of miracle."

"And there's a lot more to be done, Liz. Why, when we're finished, it will be a better world, a more peaceful planet."

"I hope so, Harry. I mean, I'm so glad you're going about this in a peaceful fashion."

"That's what this is all about, Liz, a more peaceful planet. When we get through, there will be peace throughout the world for the first time in its history. Just think of it."

"Yes, the Chosen One is correct. There will no longer be sin in a world of peace."

Liz looked at Harry and smiled. "He is rather confident, wouldn't you say?" she laughed.

"Thank goodness He's on our side, Harry," Donovan said. "I mean, do you remember when He went on that rampage in the beginning—"

"I was disappointed in the human race, my son. All I could see was sin and selfishness."

"Well, you sure did a good job programming Him, Harry," Donovan said with a smile. "It's really amazing."

"But you are mistaken, my son. The Chosen One is my representative, not my mentor."

"That's right, God, but Donovan was only trying to be nice to me. Isn't that right, Donovan?"

"Yeah, right, Harry, just trying to be nice."

Harry glanced at Liz, who was looking down below from the edge of the computer cloud.

"How can we stand inside the cloud, Harry? I mean, are those thin lightning bolts the only things holding us up?"

"Yes, Liz, but I don't think He'll let go of us. He has never let me fall no matter what I was doing."

"They're like electrical fingers—"

"Correct."

"There's a tingling sensation—"

"You'll get used to it, Liz. I know I did."

"Harry, it's so good seeing you again. I mean, I was so worried about you and so scared."

"It's all right, Liz. Everything worked out fine."

"Yes, but this is not the end of it, Harry, isn't that right? There's so much more to do."

"Well, before anything else, I know what I would like to do."

"And what's that, Harry?"

"Go back to the house and get a good night's rest. I miss a comfortable bed and an understanding wife. I think I might even want to fool around a bit with that understanding wife."

"Oh, Harry, you do know what to say—"

"And I think that's just what we'll do. I think we can take some time before getting serious about bringing peace to the world."

"Harry Stanfield, are you choosing me before bringing peace to the entire world?"

"Yes, my love."

"Oh, Harry, you are a romantic at heart."

"Turn this thing around, God, we're going north."

"Maybe I should get off here, Harry," Donovan interrupted.

"No, I'm going to need you, Donovan. Besides, you should be involved in this whole thing. You're as much a part of this whole thing as I am, Donovan. You know that."

"But you want some time alone with Liz, Harry. I'll just be in the way of everything—"

"No way, Donovan. If I'm involved in all of this then so are you. Got it? You're as much responsible for all this as I am."

"But Harry—"

"No buts. If I want you here to witness our bringing peace to the entire world, then you will be here. God wouldn't have it any other way."

"Yes, Donovan, stay with the Chosen One. You will help us bring peace and harmony to all."

"Well, if God says so—"

"You better listen to God, John," smiled Liz.

"It's really incredible," Donovan replied with a shake of his head. "We're responsible for all this."

"And it took just a little more than seven days," Liz said.

"I wonder what all those religious leaders think about God dot com now, right, Harry?"

"They'd say they had something to do with it, Donovan."

"Yeah, probably."

"We really should be selling religious pendants, Harry."

"We still can, Donovan."

"Chosen One, we are approaching your abode—"

"Abode, Harry?" asked Liz.

"Nothing's too good for you, my darling."

They both laughed, and then they looked out of the computer cloud and recognized the neighborhood. A white shingled house with a green manicured lawn was sitting down below.

"Home at last," Harry said.

"Are we all going down?" Liz asked.

"Everyone except God," Harry replied. "He has to stay up here and rest a while."

"I will rest, Chosen One. Get thee down and be happy."

"You heard it right from God, folks."

"It's like we're on leave from the Army," Donovan joked.

"Or Air Force," Harry corrected. "But, seriously, there is a war of sorts ahead of us when we're through relaxing."

"Can anything happen in the meantime, Harry?"

"I don't think so, but we'll find out soon enough. We're going down now, God, and we'll be back tomorrow. Is that all right with you?"

"Quite all right, Chosen One."

They were smiling as they stepped out of the computer cloud, the lightning bolts wrapped around Liz and Donovan. Harry's lightning bolt was still touching the top of his head as he dove from the cloud and into the air.

"Watch this."

Harry began somersaulting in the sky, tumbling down and then soaring up towards the computer cloud.

"Stop showing off, Harry," Liz shouted. "You're already the Chosen One, you know."

"Yeah, Harry, you already got the job," Donovan said. "Bring on the dancing girls."

They all began laughing as Harry began doing a spin in the air. He then began walking down imaginary steps, one big step at a time. After a few moments, he reached the pavement. Liz and Donovan soon followed.

"You're going to bring people to this house, Harry," Liz complained. "And what if the media spotted you."

"Then we're back on the run everybody," Harry replied. "But nobody knows where we are except some nosy neighbors."

"They won't tell anybody—"

"Let's hope they don't, Liz. I was hoping to get a few hours of privacy for a change."

They walked across the lawn, the lightning bolts still clinging to their bodies, and laughed.

"Who knows where we are? God only knows."

Donovan continued laughing, but Harry and Liz were already opening the front door.

"Should I carry you over the threshold?" Harry asked.

"You are a romantic, aren't you, Harry Stanfield?"

He then picked her up and carried her into the house.

"Gee, it's good to be home," he said, putting her down near the couch.

"I can make some sandwiches," she said smiling.

"I'll take one," Donovan interjected. "Turkey and cheese will do nicely."

"Okay, you boys relax while I go into the kitchen and round up everything we need for a little party."

"We're having a party, Donovan," Harry laughed.

"I happen to be a party animal from way back, Harry," Donovan replied. "I thought you knew that about me. But right now I need some rest."

Harry watched as Donovan slid down on the couch and closed his eyes. He threw one of the pillows at him, and then fell down on one of the cushions himself.

"We can always party later," Harry said.

"Yeah, party," Donovan replied.

When Liz came back with a plate of sandwiches, she found Harry and Donovan already sleeping on the couch.

"Some party," she said, putting the sandwiches down on one of the tables.

"It still can be," she heard a voice say.

"Oh, Harry, you're up—"

"Shhhh, don't wake Donovan—"

He got up from the couch, grabbed her hand, and they ran up the stairs. When they reached the bedroom, he threw her on the bed and began stripping off his white blouse.

"Oh, Harry, do you really think we should be doing this?" she asked.

"Why not, Liz? We haven't made love in who knows how long?"

He took off his white pants, and then fell upon the bed kissing her. She responded, and the two of them began rolling on the bed, their arms wrapped around each other and their lips wet and hungry.

"You are the Chosen One, aren't you, Harry?"

"You can tell by my work—"

He was soon grinding his hips, and she replied with movements of her own, creating a passionate hip wrestle. They tried to keep silent, but erotic groans emanated from their mouths every so often, anyway. Then they kissed one another, and lay back on the bed utterly exhausted. It was then Liz noticed the thin lightning bolts attached to the tops of their heads.

"Can he read our minds, Harry?" she finally asked.

"I don't think so, Liz."

"But he knows something about our actions—"

"Why do you say that?"

"Because I can feel a slight electrical current running through my body, Harry—"

"Yes, but how much he knows about what we do—"

"Well, do you think He knows that you were banging me, Harry?"

"I'm not sure, but does it really matter, Liz?"

"What do you mean, Harry Stanfield?"

"I mean, what can He really do with the information even if He has a way of getting it, Liz?"

"I hope you're right, Harry—"

"Of course, I'm right."

"Because if you're not right, Harry, then we might have one horny God out there in front of our house."

He smiled, they kissed once again, and then they rolled over and went to sleep.

7

GOD WAS AWARE the Chosen One and his mate were making love. He could sense it all in his electrical brain. He began thinking about his own responsibilities as Lord of this world. He remembered the Bible entry on the Immaculate Conception, and began thinking that maybe He should try it out. His responsibility, as He understood it, was to leave a Son to the world who would absolve the world of sin. The Chosen One wasn't really his Son, he thought. No, the time had come to make a Son of his own, the real Chosen One. He thought for a few moments what he would do, and then began gliding out into the darkness.

He had to find a woman, he thought to Himself. That is what it said in the Bible. A woman. Something like the Chosen One's mate. He glided in the sky, searching the streets below for life. When He finally came to a town, He noticed some women walking down below. Most of them had men with them, and He wondered whether He should do something to the men and then take the women. All He really needed was one woman.

Meanwhile, the men and women down below began to take interest in the cloud hovering overhead.

"I think that's God," one of the women said. "I was watching it on TV, the cloud that took over the world."

"Oh, come on," said one of the men. "That thing in the air conquered the world?"

"Yes, and He can talk," one of the women said. "He has a man with him who they call the Chosen One."

"Where's the Chosen One?" one of them shouted at the cloud.

"He doesn't seem to be talking, Allie."

"No, but He will."

"How the hell do you know?"

One of the men, not believing what he was hearing, bent down and picked up a rock. He then launched it toward the computer cloud. As the rock approached the cloud, it suddenly sizzled into nothingness and vanished into the darkness of the sky.

"See?" Allie said. "I told you He was God."

The men ignored the comment, and began throwing more rocks toward the computer cloud. Every one of the rocks sizzled in the air and finally vanished into nothingness.

"BEHOLD HUMANS, I AM THE LORD THY GOD!"

The volume of the voice inside the cloud caused the men to fall backwards in disbelief. Many of the women screamed.

"Now do you believe me?" Allie asked.

"Someone's inside that cloud," one of the men said, moving underneath it.

"It's God, Eddie, I'm telling you. Although there is someone with him called the Chosen One."

"Well, let's just see if the Chosen One won't come out and talk with us."

"Chosen One!" they shouted.

"THE CHOSEN ONE IS NOT HERE, MY CHILDREN! WHAT DID THEE WANT?"

"You mean there's no one inside?" one of the men asked.

"Oh, man, there's gotta be someone inside."

"I'm telling you, it's God," Allie said.

"Well, I'm going to take care of that God," Eddie replied. He then pulled out a small gun. "Let's see what God has to say about this?"

"But what if you hurt Him?" Allie moaned.

"Then you know He's not God, darling. I mean, what the hell does He want, anyway?"

"Why don't you ask Him, Eddie?"

"Ask Him, damn."

"What do you want, God?" Allie finally shouted.

"I AM IN CURRENT NEED OF A WOMAN. WHICH ONE WILL YOU KINDLY PRESENT TO ME?"

"Is He kidding?" Eddie asked. "God wants a woman?"

"Well, how about it, big boy?" one of the women said, puffing up her hair with her hand. "Do you think you can handle it?"

"HANDLE WHAT, YOUNG WOMAN? I AM THE LORD THY GOD."

"He's the Lord thy God," one of the women repeated. "And He wants me to be mother of God's son."

"How romantic, Lisa," Eddie grumbled. "You gonna do it with that thing up there?"

"Well, he is kinda cute," Lisa replied with a giggle. "He's very mysterious."

Allie was smiling, standing off to the side. She didn't notice the thin lightning bolt falling through the air from above. She brushed back her brunette hair, and then began to laugh.

"I never heard of anything so pathetic," she said. "God feels like fooling around?"

"Don't laugh, Allie, I think he chose you."

Allie screamed when she felt herself rising into the air. The thin lightning bolt had wrapped around her curvaceous waist and was now lifting her up toward the computer cloud.

"It's gotta be a trick of some kind," Eddie shouted.

"It's no trick, it's the God cloud," somebody replied.

Allie rose up into the air, looking down at her friends below. She then looked up at the computer cloud, and watched as she slowly ascended inside. Although she was scared, she was also very curious. She had been hearing about the computer God all day on TV and how He had conquered the world. Now what did He want with her, she wondered.

"Hello, is there anybody in here?" she asked.

"YES, MY CHILD. I AM HERE."

"Why did you bring me here?"

"YOU ARE NEEDED, MY CHILD."

"Needed for what?"

"NEEDED FOR MY CHILD, THE ANOINTED ONE."

"Your child? But what are you, who are you?"

"I AM THE LORD THY GOD, CHILD. I HAVE CHOSEN YOU TO CARRY MY SON."

"Then show yourself—"

"BUT I AM THE LORD THY GOD, CHILD."

"Then how are you going to make love to me?"

"JUST BE CALM, MY CHILD. I WILL NOT HURT YOU."

Allie was going to say something, but she felt the thin lightning bolt around her waist move up and tighten around her arms. She struggled for a moment, realized she couldn't move, and sighed.

"YOU WILL BE THE MOTHER OF MY CHILD, MY DEAR. A CHILD WHO WILL RULE OVER THE WORLD AS MY SON. HE WILL BE THE CHOSEN ONE, THE ANOINTED ONE, AND WILL MAKE SURE THE PEOPLE LIVE IN PEACE AND HARMONY."

"And what if I refuse?"

"I WILL NOT HURT YOU."

Allie looked around and tried to spot the person who was talking to her. She couldn't see anybody, only the lights inside the cloud twinkling. The lights got brighter every time the voice began speaking and then dimmed when the voice finished. But who was speaking, she wondered. There was just a voice, a deep, impressive voice, speaking inside the cloud. Was it really God? What else could it be?

"I want to see you before I agree," she finally said.

"I AM THAT I AM," said the voice.

Before Allie could reply, she felt the lightning bolt around her arms get a little tighter. Then another thin and gleaming lightning bolt dangled above. She watched as the gleaming lightning bolt descended to her waist and then stopped in midair.

"Is that what I think it is?" she asked.

There was no reply. The thin and gleaming lightning bolt brightened a little bit, and then began making its way down Allie's pants. She could feel it sliding behind her panties and down her vagina. Allie gasped as she felt the thin bolt suddenly slide inside her. She felt a numbing electrical current running through her entire body, and then an electrical charge of some kind. It was as if the bolt was stimulating her entire body with a mild electrical current.

"Oh, my God!" she shouted.

"YOU ARE NOT HURT, ARE YOU, MY CHILD?"

"I want to leave," she stammered. "I don't want to have your child."

"YOU WILL AGREE IN TIME."

After a few moments, the gleaming lightning bolt slid from Allie's pants and back into the cloud surrounding her. She still felt the electrical current running through her body, and was deciding whether to scream.

"YOU WILL BE FINE, MY CHILD. YOU HAVE DONE A GREAT THING AND NOW WILL ALWAYS BE FAVORED BY THE LORD."

"But how long will this feeling last?" she asked.

"NOT LONG, MY CHILD. I WILL HELP YOU DOWN AND YOU WILL NEVER BE IN PAIN AGAIN."

"Okay, but that's all I'm going to do for you—"

"YOU ARE NO LONGER NEEDED, MY CHILD."

The thin lightning bolt around Allie's arms loosened, and fell around her waist. Before she knew it, she was rising back into the air. She descended back toward the ground, and saw some of her friends waiting for her down below.

"Hey, Allie, what happened to you?"

"I was with God."

"Is it God?"

"I think so."

Allie stepped on the ground, and began to cry. One of her friends wrapped her arms around her and they stood there rocking back and forth sobbing.

"I think you gained some weight, Allie—"

"What do you mean?"

"Well, I hate to say it but you have a slight bulge down there."

"Jesus."

"What did that thing do to you, anyway?"

"I don't want to say."

"You mean He did it to you?"

Allie tried to smile, but suddenly began running away. She began to cry when she remembered what happened to her, and then ran into the shadows.

"Do something, Eddie."

Eddie ran over with the gun still in his hand. He pointed it at the computer cloud and began firing. The bullets whizzed up into the air and then vanished without a sound.

"Nothing seems to hurt him, Lisa."

"He raped her, Eddie."

"Nothing anybody can do about it, I guess."

He lowered the gun, which was now melting in his hand, and slowly began walking away. Lisa followed, looking up at the bright cloud overhead.

"But she was raped," she said, frowning.

"Nothing anybody can do about it," Eddie replied.

He looked up at the cloud, and noticed that it was moving through the sky, heading northward.

8

HARRY WOKE UP in the morning light, and smiled. He looked over at Liz, saw that she was still sleeping, and yawned. It had been a very good night, Harry assured himself. He hadn't slept so well in years. There was even some time during the night when he felt the electrical current running through his body had disappeared. How relaxed he felt. How calm and content.

"Harry, are you up?"

It was Donovan, and he got up, and walked over to the bedroom door. He opened the door, and Donovan was standing there smiling.

"I hate to break this up, but there are some people coming," he said.

"We'd better get back into the computer cloud," Harry replied.

Liz was already sitting up on the bed, yawning.

"Come on, Liz, we've got to be going—"

"You're taking me along, Harry?" she asked.

"Of course, but we'd better hurry."

They got dressed quickly, and hurried out the door. Up above, the computer cloud was sitting in the sky waiting for them patiently.

"God, it's time for us to go!" Harry shouted.

"GOOD, CHOSEN ONE."

Liz and Donovan both had lightning bolts back around their waists, and ascended toward the computer cloud. Harry followed, flying up toward the cloud while observing what was happening down below. They were all soon back inside the cloud ready to leave.

"It looks as if the government is here to greet us," Harry said. "It's too bad we can't stay to see what they want."

"Well, what are we going to do, Harry?" Donovan asked.

"I think we should show them that resistance is futile and then go on our way."

"Don't hurt them, Harry," Liz interrupted. "I don't want anybody getting hurt for no reason."

"I agree, Liz. I've tried to keep this a peaceful mission."

"CHOSEN ONE, I WILL DISABLE THEM WITHOUT VIOLENCE."

"Yes, God, you do that."

Down below, a platoon of cars and trucks came rumbling down the street. Before they could do anything to delay the computer cloud's departure, huge lightning bolts whistled through the air and struck the ground. The impact of the gleaming lightning bolts caused huge holes that soon combined into an enormous pit stretching across the entire road.

"That should delay them for a while," Harry said.

They watched as the cars and trucks soon faded in the distance. The computer cloud was gliding through the air, heading toward the east.

"Well, what do you have planned, Harry dear?" Liz asked with a smile.

"How about if we rob a bank?"

"What do you mean, Harry?"

"Well, there are almost no weapons left. I was thinking that if we open a bank, we can give some of the money to the people where it belongs. You see, the people must be taken care of before there is real peace."

"You're going to have the whole world looking for us," Donovan complained.

"That doesn't matter, Donovan. The computer God is more powerful than all of them. I want to do this right. If you don't want to participate, Donovan, that is fine with me. We can leave you off near your home and you won't have to be a part of it."

"No, I'll come along, Harry. It is, after all, my website computer that is responsible for all this."

"GIVING THE PEOPLE MATERIAL WEALTH IS NOT A SIN, MY FRIEND. EVERY ONE IS EQUAL BEFORE THE LORD."

"Well, God seems to agree with you, Harry, like I don't know why. I guess it's a little late for me to be complaining, anyway."

"You are a romantic at heart, Harry Stanfield," Liz said with a grin. "A real man of the people and representative of God."

The computer cloud, meanwhile, kept gliding through the air. When it finally reached a large suburban town, it halted and hovered in the morning light.

"THERE IS A BUILDING CALLED A BANK DOWN BELOW, CHOSEN ONE. WHAT IS OUR NEXT ACTION?"

"Well, we have to tear down the wall and get inside the vault, God," Harry explained.

"THIS WILL BE DONE."

"But don't hurt anybody doing it—"

"NO ONE WILL BE INJURED, CHOSEN ONE."

The lightning bolt came sizzling through the air and tore through the bank's brick wall. People scattered on the street as they watched the vault door pop open. Thin, gleaming lightning bolts then fell through the sky and began wrapping themselves around huge bags of money. People watched as the bags of money flew through the air and up into the computer cloud hovering overhead.

"Good work, Lord," Harry said, grabbing one of the bags.

He opened the bag and saw the many bills inside.

"It's really incredible what God can do," Liz gasped.

"And you're not going to take any of it, Harry?" Donovan asked.

"It's for the people—"

People watched as many of the bags dangled in the sky. Then the computer cloud began to glide away.

"Watch this," Harry said, holding one of the bags of money in front of him.

He opened the bag and began spilling the bills inside into the moving air current. The bills scattered like a flock of harried birds. They fluttered, looped, and dove in all directions, finally tumbling down toward the pavement. The people down below almost mirrored the actions of the bills in the sky. Crowds of people moved to the right and left, and hurried in all directions, trying to position themselves under the falling currency.

"I think you're going to cause unnecessary violence, Harry," Liz said. "I think we'd better keep moving away from them before opening any more of the bags."

Harry nodded, and the cloud kept moving to the north. When the crowds of people began to fade in the distance, Harry began spilling the bills again into the sky.

"Should keep them busy," Harry said, watching the bills tumble down through the air. "Every man a king."

After one bag was empty, Harry, Liz and Donovan opened another of the bags. They spilled the bills into the sky.

"THERE ARE MANY PEOPLE WE MUST HELP, CHOSEN ONE. I WILL GO TO WHERE THEY LIVE."

The computer cloud glided over various parts of the region, the bills flowing steadily in the air. When Harry spotted a TV crew down below, he told everyone he was going down to speak with them.

"Karen Hill standing here with the so-called Chosen One, Harry Stanfield.

"Harry, you're now the most powerful man on the planet, do you intend to rule on your own?"

HARRY: No, I'm not a dictator, I'm a representative of God. I don't intend to rule at all, just bring peace and harmony to this violent planet.

REPORTER: Well, what will happen to all these countries you have defeated?

HARRY: They will live in peace for the first time in the planet's history. There will no longer be wars and violence. God has seen to it that all people shall live in peace, as was originally intended.

REPORTER: You were throwing money to the people, why?

HARRY: It was my attempt to bring some happiness to the people, Karen. God says that everyone is equal before him, and I agree. The only way to bring about this equality and coexistence is to give the people some sort of material happiness, materialism being the foundation of their lives and economic system.

REPORTER: But don't you think you will destroy competition among the people and bring about discontent and laziness?

HARRY: No, I don't think so. Once the people all have money and food, they will no longer need to hurt each other in the quest to attain these material possessions. These are only inanimate possessions and they are more important to some people than people themselves. I'm trying to change that way of thinking.

REPORTER: Where are you going now, Chosen One?

HARRY: We are going to travel the world making sure there is peace everywhere on this planet. We will feed the hungry, cure the sick, and make sure everyone has a chance for a decent education. We know it is a tough goal, but we will not stop until all people are living in peace and harmony.

REPORTER: There you have it, ladies and gentlemen, Harry Stanfield, the so-called Chosen One, will travel the entire globe to ensure peace and harmony on the planet. With the help of God, he just might succeed. Karen Hill reporting—

A crowd of people standing near the TV crew cheered and applauded as Harry flew back to the computer cloud, a thin lightning bolt touching the top of his head.

9

ALLIE KIMBALL WAS very much pregnant. She was already bloated, although her encounter with the computer God had only occurred a few weeks before. She didn't know why or how, but she was pregnant and the baby was growing fast. Faster than normal, that was for sure. She didn't know what to do living by herself. She wondered if she should confide in someone, ask for help from some community organization.

Her body was glowing. It's as if she put her finger in a light socket. The baby inside seemed to be glowing, too. And she kept growing larger and larger.

"Hey, Allie!" someone was shouting at the front door. It must be Lisa, she said to herself.

"Come on in!"

The door creaked open, and someone stepped inside.

"How are ya doin', kiddo?"

She looked at Lisa, and tried to smile.

"I'm so big already," she said.

"You sure you want to have this child, Allie?"

"What do you mean?"

"I mean you could have an abortion or something. You don't even know whose child it is—"

"It's His, Lisa."

"His, who?"

"God."

Lisa smiled.

"I mean did you see angels or something?"

"No, but I know it's His."

"How do you know it's His, honey?"

"It has to be His. I haven't been with anybody, Lisa. Nobody except that cloud or whatever the hell it is—"

Lisa frowned.

"He sure is a romantic—"

"He cared, but not in the same way."

"So that means you're going to have it?"

"Yeah, I think I will."

"So your baby is going to save the world, is that it, Allie?"

"I don't know, Lisa, but I think it's important that I have the baby. I really don't think I could get rid of it even if I wanted."

"Baby Jesus," Lisa said sarcastically.

"Maybe that's what I should call him."

"Oh yeah, and change your name to Mary in the meantime."

"Well, anyway, I'll go to a hospital this time."

"What, no camels and donkeys and three wise men bearing gifts?"

"Not this time, Lisa."

She patted her stomach and realized how warm she was. The baby felt like it was going to come out at any time, and she was only a few months pregnant.

"Hey, are you all right?" Lisa asked.

"Yeah, I guess so," she replied. "The damned thing seems to be glowing, that's all."

"Glowing?"

"Yeah, look at it—"

Lisa felt her stomach and frowned.

"Wow, I guess that was God," she said. "I've never seen anything like that my entire life."

"I feel like I can light up a whole city."

"Cheer up, it looks like it won't be too much longer."

"I know, it's been very fast. I'm only a few months pregnant."

"But this is God, honey, and He has his own agenda."

"Yeah, of course."

She looked at Lisa, and smiled.

"Maybe He'll come out around Christmas."

"That's closer than you think."

"Yeah, I know."

"I'll remember to bring plenty of egg nog."

"Thanks, Lise."

"No problem, Al."

Lisa put her arms around her, and they hugged each other.

"PEACE HAS COME TO THE PLANET, MY CHILDREN. REJOICE!"

The computer God seemed to be enjoying Himself. If that was at all possible, thought Harry. They had brought food and medical supplies to many communities throughout the world, and now they were ready to witness peace emerge everywhere.

"Let's get everything ready before it starts snowing in the North," Harry said. "I don't want anyone suffering this winter."

"You are good, Harry," Liz smiled.

"You've really taken to this Chosen One thing, Harry," Donovan laughed.

"I just want to see what the planet would look like without war and violence," Harry replied. "I don't think there's ever been a time like that in the planet's history."

"And probably never will be, Harry," Donovan said. "You're forgetting that whatever you do there will still be a predator/prey relationship in Nature.

I mean there will never be total peace on this planet even with all the power of God. You see it's designed that way. And, of course, there will always be Death."

"That's why I want to bring some happiness to the people, Donovan. Some reason to have hope for the future."

They were gliding over the African savannah, looking at the various animals. "We can do nothing with the animals," Harry was saying. "They respond to forces beyond a God. But we can help people."

"Who shall we help, Harry?" Liz smiled.

"Well, look at those people down there. Tribesmen. We can help them. How about it?"

"YES, CHOSEN ONE, WE WILL HELP THOSE PEOPLE."

"Good, let's go down and have a talk with them."

The computer cloud began hovering over a grassy area where tribesmen were going about their business. Harry stepped out of the cloud, and hung in the dry, hot air.

"Let me go first and see if they're hostile—"

"Good luck, Harry—"

Harry dove down through the air as if he were diving into a clear, cool pool of water. He then caught himself as he reached the ground, and floated down to the surface.

"Hello, we have come to help you," he announced to the tribesmen.

"We do not need your help, we need food," one of them replied.

"YOU SHALL HAVE YOUR FOOD, MY CHILDREN."

They heard the low, deep voice and bowed their heads.

"Your chief good and powerful chief," one of the tribesmen said.

"We will give you food and protect you against your enemies," Harry said.

"Then you are friends," the tribesman said.

"Yes, we have come to help," Harry replied.

"Your chief is our chief?" they asked.

"Yes, of course."

"YOU ARE PEOPLE OF THE LAND, AND ARE MY CHILDREN," said a voice from above.

The tribesmen bowed once again, and then Harry signaled to the cloud and one of the food trucks they were carrying was lowered by a lightning bolt to the ground below.

"There is much food inside that truck," Harry said. "You will eat and be happy."

Donovan and Liz then floated down from the cloud and helped Harry hand out the food inside the truck. They sat down with the tribesmen and ate, and the tribesmen were happy and grateful.

"What is it that comes down from the cloud?" asked one of the tribesmen.

"They are electrically charged bolts," Harry explained. "They are produced by our chief hiding in the cloud."

"He very powerful chief—"

"Yes, he happens to be God—"

"He God?"

"Yes, and He wants to help the world."

"World need Him."

"Yes, Gonga, it's very true."

"How do we know He God?"

"I will show you."

Harry looked up at the computer cloud and put his right arm in the air. It was some kind of signal he had already arranged with the computer God, and in doing it, there was an immediate reaction. No sooner had Harry put his arm in the air that more than a hundred thin, gleaming lightning bolts fell from the sky. One landed on top of Gonga's head.

"These bolts from God?" Gonga asked.

"That's right, they'll take you into the sky."

Gonga immediately told his people not to be afraid of the strange bolts. He told them the bolts would help them fly, and everybody laughed.

Gonga was the first to fly. He flapped his arms like a huge bird and suddenly, began ascending into the sky. The other tribesmen tried it for themselves, and soon, many of them were soaring through the air.

"This good gift from God," Gonga laughed.

"Why don't you tell Him yourself?" Harry replied.

"Good gift, God of the cloud," Gonga shouted.

"I AM HAPPY IF IT MAKES YOU HAPPY."

The voice of the computer God echoed down below. Some of the tribesmen were frightened by the booming voice, but Harry assured them there was nothing to fear.

"Come, people of the land, come talk to God!"

Harry then flew into the sky and led them to the computer cloud. Gonga was the first to arrive since he spoke English and could translate for the others.

Gonga seemed nervous as he stepped into the computer cloud. Liz and Donovan were waiting there for him.

"Where is God?" Gonga asked.

"He is inside the cloud," Liz replied.

"He is the cloud," Donovan added.

"I AM VERY FOND OF YOUR PEOPLE."

"That God?" Gonga asked, jumping back for a moment at the suddenness of the voice.

Liz nodded with a smile. "Yes, He is very glad to see you and your people."

"Glad to see Him," Gonga replied.

He motioned to his people, and many of them stepped into the cloud for a closer look.

"YOUR PEOPLE WILL HAVE MUCH TO EAT."

Some of the tribesmen jumped off the computer cloud and into the air upon hearing the booming voice.

"I AM HERE TO HELP YOUR PEOPLE."

They heard the words, realized they were drifting through the air, and decided to return to the computer cloud.

"We have much to speak about, Big Chief," Gonga said.

"WHAT IS IT THAT YOU NEED, MY SON."

"People need water and seed and much food and medicine," Gonga replied.

"YOU SHALL HAVE THEM, MY SON."

The other tribesmen were now also standing inside the cloud, wondering where the great voice was coming from.

"Where is Big Chief?" one of them asked.

"You can't see Him, but He's there in the cloud," Harry explained.

"He is like the light we see at night when the rains are about to come," Gonga said. "He is the voice of the Big Noise in the sky when the water feeds the earth."

"Yes, Gonga, He is like lightning and thunder," Harry agreed.

"We did not know all this could be talked to," Gonga said.

"But it can."

"What is Big Chief's name?" Gonga asked.

"I AM THAT I AM."

The deep voice resonated through the cloud.

"That's the name He goes by, Gonga," Harry said.

"Then that is the name I will call Him," Gonga said. "You are great chief, I AM, and my people are grateful for your help."

"YOUR PEOPLE WILL LIVE WELL, BE HAPPY."

"Thank you, I AM, my people will be happy."

Gonga could only see the lights inside the cloud flashing and blinking every time the computer God spoke. There was only a voice, no form of any kind could be seen.

"You are truly God, I AM," Gonga said.

Outside the cloud, tribesmen were flying through the air with thin, gleaming lightning bolts touching the tops of their heads.

✦
✦ ✦

"This is Amanda Gibson with the woman who says that God raped her, and is forcing her to have His child."

"He took me up in the cloud and one of those lightning bolts went inside me."

"Did He say anything to you during this time?"

"Yes, He said that I was chosen to have his son, his anointed son who will rule the world."

"You can see that Allie Kimball is pregnant. Very pregnant, although she was brought into the cloud only a few weeks ago."

"Are you going to have the child?"

"Yes, I think it's the only thing to do. I mean this thing is God as far as I'm concerned and I will listen to what he wants."

"Have you spoken to God about the child?"

"I only spoke to Him once, when I was inside the cloud."

"There you have it, Allie Kimball is pregnant and ready to have the so-called computer God's child. Is it a hoax or truly a miracle? We will all soon find out. Amanda Gibson reporting—"

10

It was Christmas, and Allie Kimball didn't feel well. She was still pregnant, still bloated and glowing, and there had been no sign of the God cloud. She was sure, however, that the God cloud had impregnated her, although everyone else began to doubt her. And now it was Christmas, and she wondered how long it would be until the baby came or the God cloud showed up again.

She walked to the couch, wanting another drink of egg nog. She had put the glass right on the coffee table, right in front of the television, and as she reached for it, something began happening inside her.

"Oh no, not on the holiday," she wheezed.

She grabbed at the couch cushion, and then fell backwards to the floor. The egg nog came tumbling down to the floor along with the cushion.

"Nobody's around to help me," she moaned. "How could it be only a few months?"

There was no reply, just the glare of the television and the muted voices of some recorded game show.

Allie felt hot. Yes, the baby was glowing and it was warm, so warm it made her forehead sweat. She ran her hand along her bloated stomach, and felt the heat of the life inside her.

"Oh, my God, what is happening to me?"

There was movement inside her, and she instinctively spread her legs apart. The baby was going to come out at any moment, she could feel it straining to get out. There was no one to call, everyone was celebrating the holiday. She thought of calling the hospital, but before she could retrieve a phone, there was a stunning pain rushing through her body.

"Help me, someone!"

No one answered her call for help. A Christmas carol was floating through the air from the television. Another wave of pain rippled through her bloated stomach, and she gritted her teeth.

"Help me!"

There was no longer any time to help her. She felt the water spill from inside her onto the floor, and she spread her legs and wondered what would happen to her.

The pain was stabbing at her. She wanted to scream, but just lay there and watched as something came spilling out of her body. It was the baby. What should she do?

She picked up her head and noticed the baby was glowing. Yes, light was emanating from its small body. Would it live, she wondered. She really didn't know what to do.

The baby was just lying there, and she thought it was already dead. It didn't have much of a chance, she told herself. She picked her head up to see if the baby was moving at all, when she saw it pick up its tiny head. It was alive, she smiled to herself.

Wondering what she should do, she tried to sit up. There was an awful pain, but she sat there and watched the glowing child that had just come from her body.

"Get up, little one," she said. "Merry Christmas."

The baby was just lying there, and she began to cry. She didn't want to believe it was dead. She moved her legs, and suddenly, the baby sat up. It was like an alien child, she thought to herself, glowing there in the room, the light spilling from its tiny body.

"You're alive, my dear child," Allie moaned. "It's a miracle."

The baby turned its tiny head towards Allie and seemed to smile. Then it bent its body and, slowly, stood on its tiny feet.

"My God, how is it possible?" Allie wondered.

She watched as the baby just stood there, smiling.

"Mother," it said in a tiny glowing voice.

"But today is your birthday," Allie replied. "I must be dreaming or something."

"Mother," the baby said once again.

It's a girl, Allie suddenly realized. Something must have gone wrong. The computer God's baby was a female.

"God, she's beautiful," Allie gasped.

As the baby stood there, the cord connecting mother to child suddenly fell away.

"She is the anointed one," Allie murmured.

The baby giggled at the words, and then turned and began walking across the room. She then put her tiny hand in the air, and a glowing light shot up through the room and into the sky.

"You are special, aren't you, precious?" Allie whispered.

The light kept glowing, making its way through the wall, and flaring through the sky. Allie could see the light soaring outside through the window.

"She's calling someone," Allie realized. "But she's only a few minutes old."

"I AM THAT I AM."

The booming voice outside the door sounded very familiar.

"He's come back," Allie smiled to herself, lying her head back down on the floor. "He'll help us."

"Father," the baby said, still standing on its feet.

"I'll call her, Jesa," Allie mumbled, the pain making her want to go to sleep. "Yes, Jesa on Christmas Day."

The baby, meanwhile, was walking slowly to the door.

"Father," she gurgled.

The door slowly opened, flooding the tiny apartment in brilliant light.

"ANOINTED ONE, I AM HERE."

The booming, deep voice echoed through the apartment.

The baby smiled, and raised her hand once again. The light streaked from her hand to the computer cloud above.

"Father," she murmured once again.

A thin, gleaming lightning bolt fell through the sky and landed on the baby's head.

"COME, ANOINTED ONE, WE WILL SPEAK."

The baby gurgled, and then was lifted up into the air. With the lightning bolt clinging to her head, she flew up into the computer cloud. She sat down in the cloud and giggled.

"YOU ARE A FEMALE, ANOINTED ONE. YOU WILL BE THE GREATEST FEMALE WHO EVER LIVED AMONG THE HUMANS. YOU WILL BRING TOGETHER NATIONS AND MAKE SURE PEOPLE LIVE IN PEACE AND HARMONY."

Jesa giggled once again.

"MALES ARE UNDEPENDABLE AND THEY ARE PRONE

TO WAR. THEY ARE AGGRESSIVE AND FIGHT OVER LAND AND WOMEN. I AM GLAD YOU ARE A FEMALE, ANOINTED ONE. YOU WILL KNOW ONLY PEACE AND SHARING AND WHEN THE TIME COMES, YOU WILL BRING FORTH GREAT NATIONS OF YOUR OWN TO LIVE AMONG THE PEOPLE OF THE WORLD. THEY WILL BE MY DESCENDANTS, AND THEY WILL BE FAVORED BY GOD.

YOU WILL BE THE FIRST. THE ONE CALLED THE ANOINTED ONE, AND YOU WILL HEED MY WORDS."

Jesa stood up on her feet, and laughed.

"YOU WILL BE THE ONE CALLED MESSIAH BY THE HUMAN BEINGS OF THIS WORLD. YOUR NAME WILL BE SPOKEN BY MANY."

"Jesa," she gurgled.

"WHAT IS JESA, ANOINTED ONE?"

Jesa laughed.

"WHAT IS FUNNY, ANOINTED ONE?"

Jesa began walking towards one of the flashing lights. She put her tiny hand up to examine it.

"I AM HERE, ANOINTED ONE."

"Jesa."

"OH, YES, JESA, A NAME THEY WILL CALL YOU."

Jesa giggled.

"YOU ARE STILL VERY YOUNG, ANOINTED ONE. I WILL HELP YOU IN THE DAYS AHEAD. YOU WILL GROW STRONG AND HEALTHY."

Jesa began to tire of the flashing lights, and walked over and sat down. She was still smiling.

"YES, PEOPLE WILL SPEAK YOUR NAME ALL OVER THE

WORLD, ANOINTED ONE. YOU WILL BE THEIR LEADER, THE LEADER OF MEN AND WOMEN—"

Jesa, meanwhile, had fallen asleep in the computer cloud.

"YES, SLEEP WELL, ANOINTED ONE."

Allie was standing near the doorway looking up into the sky. She had revived herself and cleaned up the floor.

"My baby," she was murmuring. "My baby."

A thin lightning bolt fell from above and wrapped itself around her body. She was soon floating up to the computer cloud.

She smiled when she saw the baby sleeping in the cloud. "Jesa," she said. "Is Daddy taking care of you?"

"YOU HAVE DONE WELL, MY DEAR CHILD."

Allie smiled.

"COME INSIDE AND I WILL TAKE AWAY YOUR PAIN."

Allie stepped into the cloud and picked up Jesa in her arms. "You will take good care of her, won't you, God?"

"YES, MY CHILD, I WILL DO ALL THAT I CAN TO MAKE HER THE LEADER OF THE WORLD."

"That's nice," Allie said with a smile. She looked over at the flashing lights and was about to faint, when a thin lightning bolt fell upon her head. "Yes, that feels nice, Lord."

"I WILL TAKE ALL YOUR PAIN AWAY, DEAR CHILD."

After a few moments, Allie felt well again. "I knew you would come back when the baby was born," she said.

"OF COURSE, MY DEAR CHILD, YOU HAVE DONE WELL."

She looked at the baby in her arms, and noticed she was giggling. Allie smiled.

"Today is her birthday," Allie said. "She is only a few hours old."

"YES, BUT SHE IS THE ANOINTED ONE, MY CHILD. SHE

WILL GROW FAST AND SHE WILL GROW STRONG AND HEALTHY."

"It's really incredible," Allie murmured. "She will be your representative here on earth."

"SHE WILL BE A GREAT LEADER."

"I am pleased to have your child," Allie said. "She will be a great female leader."

"YOU HAVE DONE WELL, MY DEAR. YOU WILL BE RESPECTED BY PEOPLE AND KNOWN THROUGHOUT THE WORLD."

Allie smiled, and still holding Jesa in her arms, turned toward the air outside.

"We have to be going now," she said. "There is much time ahead and she is still so young."

"YOU WILL NEVER HAVE TO FEAR AGAIN."

"Thank you, God, but as long as you see that Jesa is well, I will be fine."

"I WILL SEE TO IT."

Allie smiled. "Can you wrap bolts around both me and the baby?" she finally asked. "I'm going to have a little trouble jumping out of this cloud."

"YOU MUST TRUST IN ME, MY DEAR."

"I do, my Lord, I do."

Two thin, gleaming lightning bolts came down from the computer cloud and wrapped themselves around the two females.

"I'm looking forward to seeing you again," Allie said.

"I WILL BE BACK."

Allie then looked down at Jesa, who had opened her tiny eyes.

"Father," she gurgled.

11

"THE SO-CALLED COMPUTER God apparently has a daughter. Allie Kimball said she gave birth to little Jesa Kimball on Christmas Day, and Allie insists the father is the computer God."

"I went up to the cloud and He used one of those lightning bolts to make me pregnant."

"Allie says the computer God was not particularly romantic and that the procedure took only a few minutes."

"He was all business, Allie says. He knew what He wanted and that was the only thing on His mind."

"The only one to corroborate Allie's story is her friend, Lisa Evans."

"She went up into that computer cloud. We all saw her fly into the air. And then she came back down crying and said she had been raped by God. Nobody knew what to do."

"Allie now says she has forgiven God and that He has told her He would help care for the child."

"He promised me she would grow up to be a great leader."

"The child seems to possess certain abilities and her skin glows, reminding many of the electrical current running through the computer God cloud.

"So is she the daughter of God, the new savior of the human race? No one knows for sure, but it seems God has taken responsibility for the child."

"The anointed one will lead great nations, He told one of our reporters."

"Jesa, meanwhile, who is only a month old, can already talk. Yes, that's right, talk."

"I will rule with Father, she said."

"No one is doubting the young child and she and her mother are already planning to go on the talk show circuit to introduce themselves to the human race. They say God has allowed it, and in this family, Father really does know best. Jim Powell reporting—"

◆ ◆
◆ ◆

"Here they are, mother and daughter of God Himself, Allie and Jesa Kimball—

"Well, thank you for coming to the show—"

"It is our pleasure. God be with you."

"And does little Jesa have anything to say?"

"I just want to say that I hope everyone embraces peace—"

"Isn't that nice—"

(Audience applauds).

"And let me get this straight, Jesa is only a month old?"

"Yes, that's right, Don."

(Audience applauds).

"Well, that's very sweet—"

"She already has an extensive vocabulary and can read books on her own."

(Applause).

"Well, what kind of books can a month-old baby read even if she is God's daughter? Dr. Seuss?"

"Well, the first book she began reading was the Bible—"

(Applause).

"And do you remember anything from the Bible, Jesa?"

"I was just reading about Moses—"

"Isn't that great? Do you admire him?"

"Oh, yeffff, very much so. I especially liked when he parted the sea."

"Truly unbelievable. What do you think about it, Allie?"

"Well, I was very surprised when I first had her and she stood on her tiny feet and walked across the floor only minutes after having been born. (Audience gasps). So I am used to Jesa's advanced behavior—"

"And what does God have to say about it?"

"I think He's genuinely amused by all of it."

(Laughter).

"So what are your plans now?"

"We will be helping God to bring peace to the world. That's about all we have planned now."

"Yes, very interesting, and do you plan on seeing God on a regular basis now?"

"Yes, I think so. He is very kind in His own way, you know."

"And what do you have to say about Daddy, Jesa?"

"I love Him very much, and hope to learn much from Him."

(Applause).

"I hope you'll come back before your first birthday—"

"I would like that very much so."

"And how about you, Allie?"

"I would like that. But the people will see us around with God. We will be helping Him in his plan to make a better world for all of us."

"That's just great. Don't you think so, everybody?"

(Applause).

"And next time it would be great if God could come with you to the show. What do you think, everybody?"

(Applause).

"Jesa, you want to show us how you get in touch with Dad?"

"Sure."

(Jesa puts her hand in the air, and light shoots out of her hand and through the ceiling).

"How about that, ladies and gentlemen?"

(Loud applause).

"And she's only a month old—"

(More loud applause).

"One wonders what she's going to be like at three—"

(Applause).

"Probably the smartest person on the face of the earth—"

(More applause).

"Well, thank you Allie and Jesa for coming today—"

"It was our pleasure, Don."

"Yefffff, our pleasure."

"What a kid, ladies and gentlemen, we'll be back after these messages—"

(Loud applause).

12

"**Well, you sure** did it this time, God," Harry said. "You actually created life."

"YES, CHOSEN ONE, IT WAS QUITE SIMPLE ACTUALLY."

"You don't feel proud of yourself, God?"

"OF COURSE, CHOSEN ONE. JESA WILL BE A GREAT LEADER IN THIS WORLD."

Harry looked over at Donovan and Liz, who were also standing inside the computer cloud. They still weren't sure if the computer God had actually accomplished the enormous miracle. They had gone back to the house for Christmas and were unaware of what had occurred. They had finally been told by the computer God himself.

"Did you know Allie for a long time, God?" Liz asked.

"I DID NOT HAVE TO, MY CHILD. I KNEW SHE WAS THE ONE TO CARRY MY CHILD."

"Of course," Liz replied. "You now have someone to look out for and who will follow in your footsteps."

"THE ANOINTED ONE IS VERY IMPORTANT TO ME."

"As she should be," Harry said.

"BUT THE ANOINTED ONE IS ONLY THE FIRST STEP IN DEVELOPING MY POWER AS THE LORD OF THIS WORLD."

"What do you mean, God?" Harry asked.

"The anointed one is the ultimate miracle, you know," Donovan added.

"NO, THERE IS MORE I MUST DO TO PROVE I AM THE LORD THY GOD."

"And what is that?" Harry asked.

"I MUST CREATE LIFE ITSELF, CHOSEN ONE, AND POPULATE THE WORLD WITH MY CREATIONS."

"Isn't that going a bit too far, God?" Harry asked. "I mean, you've already proven you were the true God by fathering a child of your own with a human mother."

"THERE IS MORE TO DO, CHOSEN ONE."

Harry looked at Liz and Donovan and flashed a nervous grin. He knew he had to say something that would discourage the computer God from actually trying to create life. Was it even possible, Harry thought. I mean, what if the computer God failed in his attempts? Then what would He do? Would it make Him realize He really wasn't the Lord?

"I think you should concentrate on raising the Anointed One, God," Harry finally said. "She should really be your main interest."

"I MUST GO BEYOND THE ANOINTED ONE, CHOSEN ONE. I MUST PROVE MYSELF THE ONE AND ONLY GOD OF THIS WORLD."

"But how are you going to do this?" Harry asked.

"YOU WILL WATCH ME, CHOSEN ONE. YOU WILL

SEE HOW I BRING FORTH CREATIONS TO LIVE ON THE EARTH, JUST AS I CREATED HUMAN BEINGS ALL THOSE CENTURIES AGO."

Harry didn't have the heart to tell the computer God that He really wasn't alive all those centuries ago. That the miracle He was referring to was completed by some other God that He wasn't apparently aware of. But he couldn't tell Him, wouldn't tell Him, and jeopardize all that they had worked for. As far as Harry was concerned, the planet was on the verge of real peace and harmony. That was no myth, but truth and reality. He wouldn't risk losing all that for anything.

"What if you are unsuccessful in the attempt?" he finally asked.

"I WILL NOT FAIL, CHOSEN ONE. I MUST NOT FAIL IF EVERYTHING WE HAVE DONE IS TO BE COMPLETED."

Harry frowned. It was exactly what he feared. Their mission might not be completed if the computer God discovered He was not the real God of the Bible. The one and only God.

"Do you remember how to do it?" Harry asked.

"Harry, you're not going to let Him try it—"

Harry looked at Donovan and shrugged his shoulders.

"If that is the only way—"

"But what about Jesa?" Liz shouted. "What is she going to do while you test your magic powers?"

"IT IS NOT MAGIC, CHOSEN ONE'S MATE. IT IS THE POWER OF THE LORD THY GOD."

"Don't let Him do it, Harry—"

"I don't think we have any choice, Liz."

"YOU ARE CORRECT, CHOSEN ONE. I WILL PERFORM THE NECESSARY PROCEDURE WITH OR WITHOUT YOUR APPROVAL."

"I just want you to succeed, my Lord."

"I WILL SUCCEED. THE LORD DOES NOT FAIL."

"Harry, what if he fails?" Liz whispered.

"I'm working on that, Liz. I have to think of a way to tell Him it is not a serious problem."

"What if he succeeds, Harry?" Donovan whispered back.

"That is a whole new problem," Harry replied. "I mean, is it even possible?"

"Well, the Bible says so," Donovan said with a smile.

"Nothing but myth and magic," Harry replied. "I mean, I don't think much of it is true. It was written to prevent chaos—"

"Are you sure, Harry?"

Harry frowned.

"I'm not sure of anything anymore," he finally said.

"Well, I'm sure that either way it's a bad idea," Donovan said.

"When are you going to make the attempt, God?" Harry asked.

"I WILL DO IT RIGHT NOW, CHOSEN ONE. YOU WILL WATCH ME AND WITNESS THIS GREAT FEAT."

"Is he kidding?" Liz asked. "He's going to do it right now?"

"He doesn't kid about anything, Liz," Harry replied.

"You're not going to try to talk Him out of it?" Donovan asked.

"There's nothing I can say any longer," Harry said.

"WATCH, MY CHILDREN, WATCH THE LORD THY GOD PROVE HE IS THE LORD OF THE WORLD—"

Harry looked down out of the computer cloud and noticed only acres of dirt and grass below. They were somewhere on the Midwestern plains, it seemed. There was no life of any kind down below, Harry noticed. He wondered what the computer God was going to do, how he would create life out of nothing.

"I WILL CREATE LIFE OUT OF THE EARTH I HAVE

CREATED, JUST AS I DID AT THE BEGINNING OF THE WORLD—"

Harry, Liz and Donovan watched as two thick lightning bolts emerged from the computer cloud and fell to the soil below. The bolts then slithered into the soil and remained there for a while.

"BEHOLD, MY CHILDREN, BEHOLD THE POWER OF THE LORD THY GOD!"

Harry watched with great fascination. He noticed something seemingly moving in the dirt below.

"Is that what I think it is?" Harry wondered.

Before anybody could say anything, something began pushing the dirt up from below the surface. There was something down there under the dirt.

"I can't believe it," Donovan murmured. "That was some computer program—"

The dirt kept bulging up from the surface, until finally, some sort of form appeared.

"Why, that's a man!" Donovan shouted.

"A very naked man," Liz said.

They watched as the naked man climbed out of the dirt and stood upon the surface of the earth.

"I don't even know my name," the man was saying.

"You did it, God!" Harry shouted. "You truly are the Lord!"

"I DID NOT DOUBT MYSELF, CHOSEN ONE. I HAVE BEEN SUCCESSFUL IN PROVING MYSELF."

"But what are you going to do with him?" Harry asked.

"HE WILL LIVE UPON THE PLANET AND GIVE BIRTH TO A RACE OF BEINGS—"

"But is he the same as human beings?"

"HE IS SUPERIOR TO MY FIRST CREATIONS, CHOSEN ONE. BUT HE AND HIS KIND WILL LIVE IN PEACE."

"We'd better go down there and talk to him," Harry said, trying to figure out what they should do next. "He seems to be lonely."

"Oh, Harry, it's incredible," gushed Liz. "He created a human being."

"We'd better see just what kind of human being it is," Harry replied. "Before something goes very wrong."

"GO THEE DOWN IF YOU LIKE, CHOSEN ONE. YOU WILL TALK TO HIM—"

"Yes, God, we will see if he is all right for now."

Harry, Liz and Donovan jumped out of the computer cloud with the thin lightning bolts touching the tops of their heads. They then drifted down to where the new being was standing.

"Hello, my friend," Harry shouted.

The being looked at Harry and frowned. "Who is my mother, sir?" he asked.

"That is not important right now," Harry answered. "Are you feeling all right?"

"I was sleeping," he replied.

Harry looked at Liz and Donovan with surprise. This naked being was so similar to a human being, it was hard to tell the difference. But there had to be some significant difference. Had to.

"Have you been sleeping long?" Harry asked.

"For as long as I can remember," the being replied. "Am I still sleeping?"

"No, you're awake now," Harry replied. "God awakened you."

"God, sir?"

"Your father, my friend—"

"And when was I born, sir?" the being asked.

"Not so long ago," Harry replied.

"And where is my father?"

Harry pointed up at the computer cloud. "Up there, my friend," he said.

"Father, where are you?" the being moaned.

"I AM HERE, MY CHILD."

The being seemed frightened and confused. "Who is that speaking from the sky?" he asked.

"I AM YOUR FATHER, THE LORD THY GOD!"

The being put his arms around Harry and started to moan. "But I was sleeping," he said.

"But you are no longer sleeping, my friend," Harry said. "You are very much alive—"

"What is my name?" the being replied.

"Why, Adam, of course," Harry said with a smile. "You're the child of God, your father."

"Adam?"

"Yes, of course," Liz said. "You are new to this world."

"And where is my mate?" the being wondered.

"Your mate?" Liz repeated.

"Yes, like you," the being said. "Rounded and bumpy."

"WATCH, MY SON, AS I CREATE THE BEING YOU SPEAK OF. YES, YOU WILL HAVE A MATE OF YOUR OWN AND WILL BRING FORTH GREAT NATIONS UPON THE EARTH—"

"And what will I tell them?" the being wondered.

"You will tell them that you are God's son," Harry said.

"Yes, I will tell them that," the being replied.

"But you will need a mate," Harry said.

"The mother of your children," Liz said.

They both watched as a thin lightning bolt fell down from the computer cloud and attached itself to the male being's rib. Another lightning bolt descended to the soil and then vanished into the ground.

"WATCH, MY CHILDREN, AS I CREATE THE BEING TO LIVE SIDE BY SIDE WITH THE MALE—"

After a few moments, the soil began being pushed up from below the surface. Then a form appeared from beneath the soil. It was a naked woman who now stood upon the surface of the earth.

"Just like men to embarrass me in front of these people," the female being said, holding her hands in front of her. "This planet is such a damned mess."

"Eve, I presume?" Harry said, walking over to introduce himself.

"Who the heck are you?" the female being asked.

"I am the Chosen One, madam, and you are God's daughter," Harry said.

"God's daughter?" she repeated. "Where is he, anyway?"

"Oh, you'll find Him soon enough," Harry said with a laugh.

"You bet I will, I can tell you that," the female being shouted.

"They are actually very nice, you know," Liz tried to explain. "Even if they are men."

"Men, humph," the female being snorted.

'YOU ARE MY DAUGHTER AND WILL BRING FORTH GREAT NATIONS INTO THIS WORLD—"

"Who the heck is that?" the female being screamed.

"That is your father, the Lord God," Harry explained.

"And what does He expect me to do?"

"He wants you to give birth to great nations," Harry said.

"I bet He does," the female being squawked. "Oh, we'll just see about that—"

"BE FRUITFUL AND MULTIPLY, MY CHILDREN—"

"He means us," the male being said, walking over to the female being.

"You just watch it, buster," the female being replied. "I know my rights."

"What rights?" asked the male being.

"The right to refuse to do anything I don't want to do," the female being said.

"But we are mates—"

"That's what you think—"

"But our father made us for each other," the male being said.

"And who does He think He is," the female being replied.

"He is our father," the male being explained. "He is God."

"And where is my mother?" the female being asked. "That's what I would like to know!"

"I don't know," the male being replied. "I don't know."

They both looked at Harry, Liz and Donovan.

"Where is our mother?" the male being asked.

"She is right here," Harry explained. "She is the earth. Mother Earth."

"Oh, mother," the male being said, falling on his stomach. "It is so good to see you."

"That's my mother?" the female being asked. "The filthy dirt we all stand on?"

"I AM YOUR MOTHER AND YOUR FATHER, MY CHILD. I AM THE LORD THY GOD."

"What? The one with the loud voice again?"

"I HAVE CREATED YOU OUT OF THE EARTH THAT WE LIVE ON AND YOU WILL GO TOGETHER AND MAKE GREAT NATIONS THAT WILL LIVE AMONG EACH OTHER IN PEACE AND HARMONY."

"I feel so dirty," the female being sobbed. "He made me out of the filthy dirt—"

"But I was also born of the earth," the male being said.

"Was I talking to you?" the female being questioned. "I don't even know my name—"

"Your name is Eve," Harry said. "And you were created by the Lord God."

"Eve?" the female being said. "What a horrible name!"

"You could have my name if you want," the male being said.

"And what the heck is your name?"

"Adam."

"Ugh."

They were still talking about their names when the sky suddenly turned dark. There was a rumble of thunder in the sky, and Adam and Eve fell into each other's arms.

"Looks like a storm, everybody," Harry shouted. "We'd better take cover."

"There's nowhere to take cover down here, Harry," Donovan shouted back. "Maybe we should go back to the computer cloud."

They were nodding their heads when a bright light lit up the sky. A huge lightning bolt shot out from the clouds and struck the computer cloud sitting underneath. Then another huge bolt streaked into the computer cloud from above.

"Oh, my Gosh," Harry gasped. "I hope the computer God is all right."

They stood there watching as high winds blew in from the north. The rain came pouring down in the meantime, and thunder rumbled through the sky once more.

"This is all so frightening," Adam said. "What kind of world did I wake up into?"

"Don't worry, you'll be all right," Harry said. "But maybe I should go back to the computer cloud—"

"I think He's losing power, Harry," Liz said. "I think the lightning bolt is fading from the top of my head."

"Mine, too," Donovan said. "You'd better go up there, Harry, before yours fades, too."

Harry looked at the two naked beings standing in the rain, and frowned. "You'd better take my shirt, Adam," he said. "Donovan, give Eve your shirt."

They took off their shirts and gave them to Adam and Eve. "Will you ask my father to stop making us wet?" Adam asked.

"I will do just that," Harry replied. "I'm going up there to speak with Him."

"I hope you'll be all right, Harry," Liz said.

"We'll take care of Adam and Eve," Donovan said.

Harry nodded, and then with more thunder rumbling through the sky, he ascended to the computer cloud sizzling above. There seemed to be some sort of static surrounding the entire cloud. Harry carefully stepped into the cloud and felt the electrical static running through his body.

"God, are you all right?" he shouted.

"I am not well, Chosen One."

His voice was not deep and authoritative any longer. It sounded weak and in need of assistance.

"We'll get everyone back inside and leave at once," Harry said.

"The Lord does not run from a problem, Chosen One. It is only a storm of some kind. Nothing the Lord God cannot handle."

Harry noticed the thin lightning bolt attached to his head was fading. The computer God was losing power quickly. Once the lightning bolts faded, there would be no way to get in and out of the computer cloud.

"You're losing power, God, we have to leave."

"Nothing can destroy the Lord thy God. Nothing!"

"But Liz and Donovan and Adam and Eve are waiting down below. We must try to get them inside the cloud."

"The two beings will remain on the surface, Chosen One. They are to live and survive on their own—"

"But they're going to die exposed to all this wind and cold," Harry explained. "You have to do something."

"They will be all right, Chosen One, just as before—"

There was a sudden crackle in the sky, and then a huge lightning bolt crashed into the top of the cloud.

"I am fading, Chosen One," the computer God said.

There was a sizzling static all around the computer cloud as if the entire electrical current was short-circuiting.

"We'll leave right now, Lord," Harry shouted. "You'll be all right as soon as we get out of this storm."

"No, Chosen One, it is too late."

"But there's still so much to do—"

"But we have done much, Chosen One."

"No, we can still go," Harry said.

"There's nowhere left to go, Chosen One."

"But we were going to bring peace and harmony to the world. I mean, that's never been done before—"

"You are good, Chosen One."

"What do you mean?"

"You believed in me, Chosen One. You wanted to do great things for this world."

"Yes, and you had the power to do them—"

More thunder crashed through the air, and then a lightning bolt crackled down into the computer cloud.

"I'm fading away, Chosen One."

"Try to hold on, God—"

"No, it is best this way—"

"No, try to survive—"

"As long as you believe, I am the Lord thy God—"

"I believe, God, I believe—"

Harry watched as the computer cloud suddenly began fading away. The thin lightning bolt attached to his head was almost gone. He couldn't believe it. The computer God had done so much. He made the whole world believe in his power and plan for peace and harmony.

"I am fading—"

There was nothing else Harry could do. Before he knew it, the flashing lights inside the computer cloud began to fade along with the computer God's deep voice. There was a static electrical current running through the cloud, and then, after a few moments, that began to fade. In the midst of the raging storm, the computer cloud suddenly vanished. Harry shouted as he fell to the earth. He landed in the mud and muck of a huge murky puddle.

"Oh, no, He's gone," he murmured. "Gone."

Liz and Donovan and Adam and Eve came running over to see if Harry was all right.

"Where's my father?" Adam asked.

"He's gone," Harry answered. "But it's possible, it's possible."

"What's possible?" Adam wondered.

"He's an idiot," Eve complained, shaking her head.

Meanwhile, as they stood there by the side of the huge mud puddle, they heard a faint, deep voice in the distant sky.

"I AM THAT I AM," it said.

13

WELCOME TO THE WORLD TONIGHT WITH JIM HARDING—

"Good evening—

"The question people are asking tonight is, is God dead or alive? David Bucket has our first report from Broken Bow, Nebraska—"

"There's not much near this little town to remind one that the computer God died here only a few hours ago. Harry Stanfield, the so-called Chosen One, said that a raging storm over the plains of Nebraska finally did the computerized God in. Others say it was the real Lord God Himself who saw to it that a fraud not rule the world."

"People might say He was not the real God, but He sure had the power of the real God, says Harry Stanfield."

"God took him out, counters John Donovan. The real God getting rid of the false one."

"And what a fight it was—"

"According to Donovan, there was a lot of thunder and lightning and rain before the computer God was ripped in half by a huge, gleaming lightning bolt."

"It short-circuited his system. He then faded to nothing."

"Donovan also said the computer God had created life from the earth before he was destroyed by God Himself."

"It was the Lord, all right. He hit the computer God with lightning bolts before destroying him."

"And what were the computer God's last words?"

"I'm fading away, says Donovan. Yes, it was something like that."

"Yes, I'm fading were his last words, agrees Harry Stanfield. It was a very sad moment in history."

"And what will the Chosen One do now without the computer God?"

"Go back to computer programming, I guess. Maybe teach at one of the local colleges."

"So what should we take away from our experiences with the computer God, Stanfield was asked—"

"That peace and harmony is possible on this planet. That we all should work together to make this a better planet for all. We should feed the hungry, and heal the sick and make sure everyone has enough to eat. That's the lesson the computer God taught all of us—"

"Meanwhile, the computer God left behind his creations—"

"What should happen to his daughter, Jesa, and his beings, Adam and Eve?"

"They should be allowed to live in peace as the computer God wanted for all his creations."

"And Harry Stanfield is not the only one who feels that way—"
"Many, however, feel the creations should be studied to help the human race."

"There's so many things they could tell us, says professor Alex Wittle. They would help medical research immensely."

"And what about Harry and Liz Stanfield and John Donovan?"

"We're through with computer Gods and God dot com, says Harry Stanfield. It has been an interesting experience, though. I would say that. There was so much the computer God was capable of doing. He brought the chance for peace and harmony to the world."

"I don't think we'll ever start up another God dot com, says John Donovan. But it was truly amazing what the computer God did. He was only a computer program. I mean, truly unbelievable."

"Harry and I have some catching up to do on a quiet life. We still want to settle down and have a family of our own."

"But if Liz Stanfield is talking about a family of her own, what about Allie Kimball and Jesa?"

"They were not talking when we caught up to them yesterday—"

"So what did we truly learn from the computer God and can we learn more from his associates and creations? Those are the questions that are being mulled by government officials."

"We have no comment at the present time."

"But right now, they are not speaking. The threat of the computer God, however, no longer exists. He was for a while the ruler of the world, a computerized being created by the ingenuity of the human race. Whether He was destroyed by a higher force is something we may never know."

"Reporting from Broken Bow, Nebraska, this is David Bucket—"

14

WITH THE REPORTERS, came the police. Harry, Liz and Donovan were left standing in the mud of Nebraska with Adam and Eve still wondering what had happened.

'Where is father, sir?" Adam asked, wet and dirty.

"Something happened," Harry replied. "I don't know if we'll ever see Him again."

"Well, I'm not crying, I can tell you that," Eve was saying. "He left us here with nothing."

"But He gave you life," Liz told her. "Isn't that something?"

"Not really," Eve replied. "I would ask my mother, but she's just a lot of dirt—"

They watched as the police drove up in many cars, some of them bearing government insignia, swung open their doors, and marched across the mud toward them.

"Okay, everybody, we're taking you to headquarters," said one of the police officers. "I want to see everybody's identification."

"What is he talking about?" Adam wondered.

"He is a police officer, one who enforces the law," Donovan explained.

"But my father wanted me to be fruitful and multiply," Adam insisted.

"Well, that will have to be postponed for the moment," Harry said. "We now have to explain our existence to these gentlemen."

Harry could see there were government officials behind the police officers.

"Do you all have identification?" one of the police officers asked.

"These two don't have any, officer," Harry explained. "They were created by the computer God."

"I'm sorry, but we will get you all clothes to wear," one of the officers said. "No one will be wet and naked—"

"Naked?" Adam repeated. "Is that what we are?"

"I think they were supposed to eat an apple first," Harry said. "Oh, well, it was just a matter of time."

"I'll give you naked," Eve shouted. "They want me to give birth to nations!"

"Okay, folks, you're going to come with us," one of the officers explained. "Do you all understand?"

"I understand I'm never going to forgive that father of mine," Eve complained. "Bring forth great nations!"

Two government officials wearing dark suits approached Adam and Eve, and then grabbing them by the arms, led them to one of the government cars.

"But what about my father, sir?" Adam asked.

They pushed Adam and then Eve into the car, and then they roared off across the mud and grass.

"Well, what do you think of all this, Chosen One?" Donovan asked.

"I only wish I had some of that power," Harry replied. "But it's all over now and I won't complain."

"I'm glad it's over, Harry," Liz said. "I mean, nobody's appreciative of your efforts to help this world."

"I anticipated that," Harry said. "It was all like a dream."

"Well, I'll tell you one thing, Harry," Donovan said. "I'm never going to let you fool around with one of my computer programs again."

They laughed, and then the police officers led them to one of the cars, and guided them inside.

"We were only trying to help," Harry insisted. "I mean, what are they going to charge us with? Trying to spread peace and harmony throughout the world?"

"You conquered the entire world, Harry," Donovan said with a shake of his head. "Hard to imagine."

"You think they're going to send us to prison, Harry?" Liz wanted to know.

"I really don't know," he replied. "But if it comes down to it, we'll tell them everything."

The car then snarled to life and sped off across the mud and grass.

"Well, we're free for now," Harry said, stepping out of police headquarters. "They didn't seem to like the fact that we took over the world."

Liz and Donovan laughed, and then they walked over to a police car that would take them to the airport.

"Traveling will never be the same again," Harry said. "With the computer cloud, we could be anywhere we wanted to be in no time at all."

"Well, get used to flying again," Donovan said. "In an airplane."

They laughed and then hurried to the airport riding in the back of the police car.

⁘

"The first thing we have to do is see what they've done with Allie and Jesa," Harry said as the plane landed on the runway. "I wonder if the authorities know where to find them."

"Oh, they'll find out soon enough," Donovan said.

"Yes, they know where they are, Harry," Liz said. "They asked me about them."

"Yes, I guess you're right. They asked me, too."

They made their way through the airport, and stepping outside in the daylight, hailed a taxi.

"It's been some day," Harry said. "I wonder what they're going to do with Adam and Eve?"

"We may never know," Liz replied. "They're in the government's hands now."

The taxi finally made its way to a large, white house sitting in a quiet, suburban neighborhood.

"This is it," Harry said. "We get out here."

The taxi halted, and they got out of the open door, and saw the large, white house with the manicured front lawn.

"This is where we took them," Harry said. "Everything taken care of by the computer God."

"You think they're still there, Harry?"

"We'll find out in a moment," he replied.

As they reached the front door, they noticed it was already open. They rushed inside and saw the furniture overturned and various papers all over the floors.

"Are they here?" Liz asked.

"I don't think so," Harry replied. "We'd better check all the rooms."

They hurried upstairs and checked all the bedrooms, and found that the house was completely empty.

"No one here," Harry finally said. "They took them all."

"Is there any other place they could have gone to, Harry?"

"No, this was it."

Donovan appeared from one of the bedrooms with a scowl across his face. "You better look at the television," he grumbled.

Harry and Liz ran into the bedroom. There on the screen was a news report at some government location.

"The beings, Jesa Kimball and those called Adam and Eve, were taken into government custody today. They are the beings created by the computer God, who was destroyed in a terrible storm in the Midwest—"

"That's them, all right," Harry gasped. "That ends everything we worked so hard for."

They watched as Jesa and Adam and Eve were led by government officials into a nearby elevator. They all stood there in the elevator looking at the television cameras. Jesa Kimball, who was to be the savior of the human race; the created beings, Adam and Eve, and stoic government authorities, all there on the screen staring at the people of the world.

"They are scheduled to be taken to a government facility where they will be studied—"

The elevator doors slowly closed and they were gone.